TALKS WITH THE MASTERS

Conversations with

Isaac Asimov
Ray Bradbury
Arthur C. Clarke
James Gunn

TALKS WITH THE MASTERS

GEORGE ZEBROWSKI

Edited by
Pamela Sargent

WILDSIDE PRESS

Published by Wildside Press LLC.
wildsidepress.com

INTRODUCTION
by Pamela Sargent

George Zebrowski and I were college freshmen when we met, still in our teens, but George already knew that he was going to be a writer. Specifically, he wanted to be a science fiction writer. I was an aspiring writer myself, but had only a vague idea of how to go about becoming one. George, however, had actually met some of the writers he so admired, including such luminaries as Arthur C. Clarke and Isaac Asimov, whose example and encouragement inspired him to achieve his ambition. Much later, after more than three decades of being a professional science fiction writer himself, George interviewed four of the authors whose work and whose example had inspired him.

Or, as George puts it, "I encountered the gods of my youth as a colleague." This book is the result of those encounters.

* * * *

Isaac Asimov was born on January 2, 1920, in Petrovichi, Russia. He immigrated with his family to the United States as a toddler, grew up in Brooklyn, New York, and became a biochemistry professor at the Boston University School of Medicine while pursuing writing. A prolific writer who published nearly five hundred books, he was the author of the science fiction classics *I, Robot,* the *Foundation* trilogy, *The Caves of Steel*, *The Naked Sun*, and the Nebula and Hugo Award-winning *The Gods Themselves.* He also published nonfiction on a wide variety of subjects, among them astronomy, biology, math, religion and literary biography. (George claims that it was Isaac's *The Intelligent Man's Guide to Science*, later revised as *Asimov's Guide to Science*, that helped get him through the dreaded New York State Regents science exams in high school.) Asimov died in New York City on April 6, 1992.

Like Asimov, George was also an immigrant to the U.S., arriving with his parents in the early 1950s and growing up in New York City (Manhattan and the Bronx, his residence in those two boroughs separated by a year and a half in Miami, Florida). About his first meeting with this writer whom he'd been reading for years, he writes:

> I first met Isaac Asimov at the World Science Fiction Convention of 1963, held in Washington, D.C. I had seen him at various gatherings since 1960, but had not had the courage to approach him. Now, not quite eighteen, I was so overwhelmed by my recent reading of the Foundation trilogy that I stumbled over my words as I shook his hand.
>
> "Er, would…you ask me a question?" I asked, inadvertently baring the ego of a would-be writer.
>
> "Of course!" he shouted at once, delighted by the opening I had given him. "What would you like me to ask *you*?"
>
> I went red and my knees shook, and he seemed to enjoy my consternation mightily. I had expected to meet the austere Hari Seldon and to feel the exhilaration of reason that was for me the great distinguishing feature of Asimov's work: I had not expected to meet an ebullient Hari Seldon. A moment passed. I felt relieved, and a bit flustered, when Isaac's knowing smile turned into a kindly gaze.

In the years to follow, George, often with me tagging along, spent time with Isaac at various conventions and events, including the 1972 Nebula Awards Banquet held in New York City in the spring of 1973 (Berkeley, California and New Orleans, Louisiana were the sites of two other Nebula banquets that took place simultaneously), where Isaac won his first Nebula Award, given by the Science Fiction Writers of America (now the Science Fiction and Fantasy Writers of America) for *The Gods Themselves*. Although he was honored earlier in 1963 with a special Hugo Award for his science essays in *The Magazine of Fantasy & Science Fiction* and another Hugo for Best All-Time Series for the Foundation trilogy in 1966, this was his first major SF award for a single work. We were with a small group who joined Isaac for drinks after the awards ceremony, which was, as George recalled, both a triumphant and melancholy event for the winner:

...Isaac called to me from across the emptying banquet hall. Startled, I waited for him to approach.

"This is it—the end, George," he said.

"What do you mean?" I replied.

He held up his award trophy. "I've reached the top,"

"I'm sure you'll win another," I said. My words did not seem to cheer him as he wandered away.

In time I learned what a quagmire human nature and humans are, but it still seems to me that we need the exhilaration of reason to cut through to better circumstances for our kind; I must confess that it saddens me how few of my fellow humans have this feeling for reason, but then even Hari Seldon must have had his despairing moments.

And as it happened, Isaac was still far from reaching the top. Ahead of him were having his books on the *New York Times* bestseller list, more Nebula and Hugo Awards, an asteroid named in his honor in 1981 (5020 Asimov), and a movie based on his award-winning novelette "The Bicentennial Man" starring Robin Williams, to name only a few of the high points.

In 1983, George collaborated with Isaac and prolific anthologist Martin H. Greenberg on a major anthology, *Creations: The Quest for Origins in Story and Science* (Crown, 1983). And in the late 1980s, George had the opportunity to write about one of his favorite Asimovian characters, Hari Seldon, when he was invited to contribute a story to *Foundation's Friends*, an anthology in honor of Isaac Asimov with original stories using characters and settings created by Asimov. George remembers working on that story, "Foundation's Conscience," this way:

> I discussed "Foundation's Conscience" with Isaac by phone as I was writing it, and some interesting ideas came up—one being that artificial intelligence, not sharing human evolution and psychology, would be free of Hari Seldon's psychohistorical laws and might be able to strike out in new directions, perhaps according to psychohistorical laws of their own, with a relatively greater degree of freedom than humankind had ever had. Isaac seemed struck by this idea, and I imagined that it might play some role in the last Foundation book. I feel now that Isaac came by and asked me to

come play in his backyard for a while. The pleasure and sureness I felt in writing "Foundation's Conscience" reveal to me the pervasiveness of his influence on my early character and later writing life.

George was offered the chance to interview Isaac in 1990 and conducted the interview by mail, telephone, and in person at Isaac's apartment in Manhattan. Isaac died soon after completing the interview and was eulogized at a memorial service on April 22, 1991 at the Society for Ethical Culture's building on Central Park West.

"Now that he is gone," George wrote later, "I realize that I knew Isaac for nearly thirty years, and he was my friend and colleague for the second half of that time. A harsh word never passed between us. The door of his home was always open to me, and I wish that I had taken up his standing invitation more often. In the 1980s, when a publisher had mistreated me, Isaac immediately went to my defense. He did not waste a single moment, and his help was effective; and he gave me his help even as his health was failing. When I went to see my friend…to complete this interview, I was shaken by his declining health. Isaac put on a brave face as he answered my final queries. He paused to answer the phone several times during our conversation, and each time, despite his obvious discomfort, his voice was clear and strong, his words rational—the voice of the father figure (Hari Seldon himself!) who helped me to think for myself and become the writer I am. One thing is certain: he will always be with us, because he wrote so much that I will be reading him for the rest of my life, and for that I am grateful."

* * * *

Ray Bradbury was born on August 22, 1920, in Waukegan, Illinois, As a child, he was an avid fan of both magicians and fantasy fiction, especially the works of L. Frank Baum, Jules Verne and Edgar Rice Burroughs. His use of his childhood experiences in the Midwest in some of his novels and stories accounts for the nostalgia that characterizes much of his work even when he was writing about the future.

Bradbury's family moved to Los Angeles, California, in 1934, where he finished high school but couldn't afford to go to college;

instead, he educated himself in libraries. As he has said, "Libraries raised me. I believe in libraries because most students don't have any money. When I graduated from high school, it was during the Depression, and we had no money. I couldn't go to college, so I went to the library three days a week for 10 years."[1]

In 1937, he joined the Los Angeles Science Fiction League and his early writing was encouraged by Henry Kuttner, Edmond Hamilton, Robert A. Heinlein, and Leigh Brackett, successful writers who became his friends and mentors. Many of his early stories were published in *Weird Tales*, but unlike most other SF writers, Bradbury went on during the 1940s to publish stories in magazines like *Collier's*, *Harper's*, *McCall's*, and *The New Yorker* while continuing to contribute to the genre and pulp magazines he loved. His major works include *The Martian Chronicles*, *Fahrenheit 451*, *The Illustrated Man*, *Dandelion Wine*, and *Something Wicked This Way Comes*, while *Green Shadows, White Whale* was his semi-fictional account of his experiences working on the screenplay for director John Huston's 1956 motion picture adaptation of Herman Melville's *Moby-Dick*. Bradbury's many honors included the World Fantasy Award for Lifetime Achievement, the National Medal of Arts, a Pulitzer Prize Special Citation, the Bram Stoker Award for Lifetime Achievement in horror fiction, and the SFWA Grand Master Award for his science fiction.

Those growing up in the U.S. of the 1950s and 1960s were likely to have encountered Ray Bradbury or his work in some fashion, whether or not they realized it at the time and even if they weren't fans of SF or fantasy fiction. Rod Serling's *Twilight Zone* TV anthology series reflected Bradbury's influence; even though only one of Bradbury's *Twilight Zone* scripts, "I Sing the Body Electric," was produced for the original series, Serling openly acknowledged his influence, while Bradbury was a friend and colleague of Richard Matheson, Charles Beaumont, and George Clayton Johnson, all of whom wrote memorable *Twilight Zone* episodes. *Fahrenheit 451* and *The Illustrated Man* became movies and Bradbury himself was one of the commentators who appeared on news broadcasts with CBS anchorman Walter Cronkite during the first moon landing in 1969.

1   "Despite Ray Bradbury's Efforts, A California Library Closes," Jennifer Steinhauer, *The New York Times*, December 9, 2009.

George has strong memories of reading *The Martian Chronicles* when he was in his early teens and a patient for many months at the Hospital for Special Surgery in Manhattan. The influence of Bradbury showed him that poetry as well as reason could enrich science fiction, and if Bradbury often ignored scientific facts, his writing transcended the genre and became an often nostalgic, often dark, unclassifiable science fantasy. Bradbury the person was to remain a more distant figure, at least geographically. Had his parents decided to settle in Los Angeles instead of New York City, perhaps Bradbury would have become an early mentor to George.

In 1989, George and I both finally met Ray Bradbury in person at the Nebula Awards ceremonies and banquet in New York City, where Ray was honored with the SFWA's Grand Master Award and a reception in his honor was sponsored by Bantam Books, which had just published his Knopf collection of short fiction, *The Toynbee Convector*, in paperback. He turned out to be a robust and gregarious man with a warm smile and thick white hair, and it was after that meeting that he and George began to correspond and exchange phone calls. George later reprinted a Bradbury story, "The End of the Beginning," in *Skylife*, an anthology he edited with Gregory Benford, and interviewed Ray by phone in 2004.

On June 5, 2012, Ray Bradbury died at the age of 91 in Los Angeles. Beginning in 2010, the Ray Bradbury Award for Outstanding Dramatic Presentation, a category that includes movies, television, internet, and stage productions, has been presented annually by the Science Fiction and Fantasy Writers of America.

* * * *

Although he lived for most of his adult life in Sri Lanka (formerly Ceylon), Arthur C. Clarke was born in the southwest coastal town of Minehead, England, on December 16, 1917, to a farming family. After his father's death, unable to afford a university education, he moved to London in 1936, took a government job, and became a member, and eventually the chairman, of the British Interplanetary Society.

In summarizing the many accomplishments of the influential writer who was to become Sir Arthur C. Clarke, George wrote:

It's hard to know where to begin detailing this SFWA Nebula Grand Master's career... After a number of significant moments in his early life (well documented in *Arthur C. Clarke, The Authorized Biography*, by Neil McAleer, Contemporary Books, Chicago, 1992), he went on with the aid of a grant to King's College in London, from which he was graduated in 1948 with first class honors in physics and mathematics. He was Chairman of the British Interplanetary Society and was a member of the Academy of Astronautics and other scientific bodies. As an RAF officer during World War II he was in charge of the first radar talk-down system tests. His novel *Glide Path* (1963), which he is fond of describing as his only non-science fiction novel, is based on his early experiences with radar. The novel is a kind of reverse science fiction, and would have been SF if he had written it in 1940. It contains all the insights and prophetic passages to be found in Clarke's works of foresight, fiction and non-fiction.

Clarke's nearly one hundred books have been translated into more than thirty languages. His many awards and honors include the UNESCO Kalinga Prize for science writing (previous winners have been Bertrand Russell and Julian Huxley); the AAAS-Westinghouse science writing prize; the Bradford Washburn Award; and the Hugo, Nebula, and John W. Campbell Memorial Awards—these last three, the triple crown of science fiction awards, for *Rendezvous With Rama* (1973). Stanley Kubrick and he shared an Oscar nomination in 1968 for the movie, *2001: A Space Odyssey*. In 1981 Clarke received an Emmy for his contribution to satellite communications. *Arthur C. Clarke's Mysterious World*, a thirteen-part television series, has been seen in many countries, as has the subsequent series *Arthur C. Clarke's World of Strange Powers*; but he became a television figure much earlier by joining Walter Cronkite during the CBS coverage of NASA's space missions and the Apollo lunar expeditions from 1957-1970.

Clarke's engineering depiction, in 1945, of communications satellites earned him the 1982 Marconi International Fellowship; the gold medal of the Franklin Institute; the Vikram Sarabhai Professorship of the Physical Research Laboratory, Ahmadabad, India, and a 1994 Nobel Peace Prize nomination. He was also the Chancellor of the University of Moratuwa, near Colombo, Sri Lanka, where he made his home until his death on March 19, 2008.

His well-known novels include *Childhood's End*, *The City and the Stars*, *The Deep Range*, *Earthlight*, *Imperial Earth*, *2001: A Space Odyssey*, *The Fountains of Paradise*, and *The Songs of Distant Earth*. His most important nonfiction includes *Profiles of the Future*, *The Promise of Space*, and *Ascent to Orbit* (a collection of his technical papers). Other novels are *The Hammer of God*, *The Ghost from the Grand Banks*, and *3001: The Final Odyssey*.

This man, whose influence on our planetary culture is comparable to that of H. G. Wells, has been described "as a multifaceted, divided man, but this is illusion. Clarke is whole; it is our culture that is divided. More than any other SF writer, Clarke truly lives in the interzone between science and literature. His career has been a deliberate struggle to make this no-man's-land a place worth living and working in. And he has made both sides respect him on his own terms."

I can only add that the culture of literary criticism, on the whole, still does not know how to write about Clarke without referring to myths and metaphors, rather than to knowledge and possibility, while the scientific culture perhaps fails to value his fiction enough.

Clarke was often in New York City for extended periods, which was how George was able to meet him, an encounter he wrote about in the anthology *Sentinels in Honor of Arthur C. Clarke* (Hadley Rille Books, 2010), edited with Gregory Benford, which collected fiction influenced by Clarke's work and nonfiction about Sir Arthur's writing. George recalled their first meeting this way:

In early October 1961 I attended the American Rocket Society's gathering at the New York Coliseum. This was an open exhibition of the history and current state of space technology. I wandered around, clutching my copy of *Booster*, the Society's daily newsletter, marveling at how much there was to see. One booth showed a short film about Sputnik. I still remember the chills this brief film sent through me even half a decade after the launching of the first Earth satellite. Then I drifted over to an exhibit of spaceship designs.

"That's a Clarke Moonship," someone said next to me, and my ears turned like radio dishes toward the familiar sound of the name.

"And that's Clarke himself," the voice added.

"Where?" I asked.

"Right there, next to you."

I turned with disbelief and saw a sandy-haired gentleman bending down to examine a picture of a Lunar spacecraft. He looked exactly like the photograph on the back jacket of *The City and the Stars*. I said hello in a daze, introduced myself, and managed a few words about reading his novels. He signed my copy of *Booster* …and suggested that I attend a reception that evening. At that gathering Clarke met me at the door, took me inside, and introduced me to Willy Ley (whose books I knew), and to Wernher von Braun, who asked me, "What are you going to be, young man?"

"A writer," I replied uneasily.

"Good, good," he said. Awed and a bit afraid, I forgot to have him sign my copy of *Booster*.

This was too much for a high school student. I had not expected to meet any of these people. I lost all track of time, was late in getting home, and got a tongue-lashing from my stepfather, but I didn't much care. I had met Arthur C. Clarke!

After that first meeting, George and Arthur kept in touch with letters, phone calls, and occasionally in person at events such as the 1972 Nebula Awards banquet in New York, where Arthur received the Nebula Award for his novella "A Meeting with Medusa." After George's novel *Macrolife* (Harper & Row, 1979) was published, Clarke broke his rule of not commenting on novels with promotional quotes to offer the following blurb for *Macrolife*'s paperback edition: "It's been years since I was so impressed. *Macrolife* manages an extraordinary balance between the personal and cosmic elements. Altogether a worthy successor to Olaf Stapledon's *Star Maker*. I'm confident that George's book doesn't need any recommendation from me. You can quote that! One of the few books I intend to read again."

George recalls: "When Arthur was voted the Nebula Grand Master in 1986, I had the pleasure of including a story of his in *Nebula Awards 21*, which I edited. Appropriately, Clarke's words of acceptance of the honor, for publication in the anthology, arrived via a satellite computer-data transmission link from Sri Lanka."

The interview here was conducted by phone, email, snailmail, audio tape, and in person in New York City. "It was completed in March of 2000," George later wrote, "with follow-ups through the end of the preceding year, most notably in early October of 1999, at the Chelsea Hotel, where Sir Arthur greeted me and writer/scientist Charles Pellegrino with the warmth of a family member and the playful wit of a friend, in between visits from Walter Cronkite, Woody Allen, Rupert Murdoch, and many other notables, while vigorously fielding phone calls from the United Nations and other insistents who had learned of his presence in the United States."

George adds: "My friend is gone, and I am reminded of his saying that if you listened to him about the near future, you would go broke; but if you failed to take his longer view, your descendants would go broke. In his last days, Arthur wished to be remembered primarily as a writer."

* * * *

James Gunn was born on July 12, 1923, in Kansas City, Missouri. He earned a B.S. degree in journalism in 1947 after three years in the U.S. Navy during World War II, and his M.A. in English in 1951, both from the University of Kansas. He also did graduate work in theater at KU and Northwestern. In 1969, at the University of Kansas, he taught one of the early university courses in science fiction. He began writing and publishing science fiction in 1948, has published more than one hundred pieces of short fiction, and is the author of the novels *Station in Space, The Joy Makers, The Immortals, The Listeners, Kampus,* and *The Millennium Blues.* His most recent novels are a trilogy: *Transcendental* (2013), *Transgalactic* (2016), and *Transformation* (2017). Gunn is also an anthologist; his highly praised six-volume series of anthologies, *The Road to Science Fiction,* covers the development of science fiction from the Sumerian epic Gilgamesh through the 1990s. He has also won praise as a teacher and scholar in the field—he was one of the first in the U.S. to teach SF at the college level—and is the founder of the Gunn Center for the Study of Science Fiction at the University of Kansas, where he taught for many years and where he continues to oversee the Center. He has been honored with SFWA's Grand

Master Award and inducted into the Science Fiction Hall of Fame in Seattle, Washington (as were Isaac Asimov, Ray Bradbury, and Arthur C. Clarke).

And, as both George and I were to discover during all the years we've known Jim, he is also a thoroughly good person, a considerate and attentive mentor, a friend who always has your back, and one of the fiercest and most influential advocates for science fiction as a literary form.

Writing about his accomplishments in 1995, in the magazine *Science Fiction Age*, George had this to say:

> James Gunn has not been neglected as an historian and critic of SF, but these accomplishments have diverted attention from his exceptional fiction. In 1958, at the dawn of the space age, Gunn's story "The Cave of Night" reached the center of popular culture when it was presented as a teleplay by *Desilu Playhouse*, with E.G. Marshall as the scientist and Lee Marvin starring as the astronaut. The story was part of Gunn's remarkable *Station in Space* (1958), a novel about the lives of astronauts during the early years of solar system exploration that not only catches the ambivalence of culture and politics to space exploration and foreshadows later 1960s skepticism about the Moon program, but also presents space travel grimly, realistically, even mockingly—looking forward in certain ways to Barry N. Malzberg's later cycle of stories and novels about astronauts...
>
> Of Gunn's more than twenty other books, *The Joy Makers* (1961) has an icy clarity and a seductive plausibility that puts it at the top of the sociological school of SF that flowered in the 1950s. *Star Bridge* (1955), written with Jack Williamson, is a colorful space opera, filled with exciting imagery. *The Listeners* (1972) is still the definitive novel about radio contact with an alien civilization.

By the 1950s, James Gunn was well on the way to creating a body of work comparable to that of writers such as Ray Bradbury, Arthur C. Clarke, and others who were to become iconic SF writers, and yet, along with a number of other equally gifted writers of that time, he somehow didn't achieve the instant name recognition of an Asimov or a Clarke. In his introduction to a hardcover reprint of Gunn's 1961 novel *The Joy Makers* (Classics of Modern Science Fiction series, Crown, 1984), George speculated about possible reasons for this relative neglect and cited "the use of irony" by Gunn as one possibility: "Great popularity in the writing of fiction is not won by being ironic; the tone is instantly picked up by the unthoughtful, and disliked while being misunderstood; thus a work's incisive, often comic, view of humanity is missed…Yet, as with *Gulliver's Travels*, which much of the public still thinks of as a children's book (to avoid considering its uncomfortable view of humanity), these works of science fiction have a better chance of being thought worthy decades from now than do the sentimental, naively heroic adventures which are aimed at adolescents."

Or maybe it was just luck, which also has much to do with who is remembered and who is forgotten.

As it happens, the reputation of even the most iconic SF figures of the past has faded. The genre, to its credit, has become far more diverse, enriched by writers of various identities, and is far more embedded in popular culture, given that we are all living in the kind of science fictional world envisioned by earlier writers, but it is also more fragmented. Once treasured classic works drop out of sight while subgenres proliferate. Once most of the writers and editors in the field were at least aware of one another and familiar with most of the books and stories being published; now it's increasingly hard to keep track of them all.

But Jim Gunn remains, as one of his former students, award-winning writer John Kessel, points out, one of the unifying threads "in the development of science fiction. As a boy, he shook hands with H.G. Wells. In the late 1940s he sold fiction to John W. Campbell and throughout the 1950s he was a regular in Horace Gold's *Galaxy*, becoming a mainstay of the movement toward sociological science fiction. He was one of the first people ever to study science fiction in the academy, writing an M.A. thesis on SF, portions of which were published in *Dynamic Science Fiction* in 1953. His first novel was a collaboration with Jack Williamson that the *New York Times* said read like a collaboration between Asimov and Heinlein."[2] Not only does Jim's body of work provide these

2   John Kessel, "James Gunn, Grandmaster," http://www.sfcenter. ku.edu/Kessel-appreciation.htm, accessed May 1, 2018. The quotation is from a speech delivered at the 2007 Nebula Awards ceremony in New

connections, but his influence, through the Center he founded, his scholarship, and his teaching, has also been more far-reaching than even die-hard SF readers may realize. Among his notable students who are now among some of the prominent writers of SF are John Kessel, Pat Cadigan, Bradley Denton, Kij Johnson (Associate Director of the Gunn Center and now teaching at the University of Kansas), and Christopher McKitterick, the Center's Director, to name only a few. An annual conference, at which the John W. Campbell Award for best SF novel and the Theodore Sturgeon Award for best SF in short fiction are presented, attracts writers and editors from around the world to the KU campus; George and I have been to three of these conferences and found them among the most stimulating and inspiring experiences of our lives as writers. The Center also offers writing workshops and courses in the history of SF based on Jim's groundbreaking work, thus ensuring that his influence will persist. I suspect that if one were to trace all of Jim's connections to those involved with SF as writers, editors, and readers, there would be very few untouched by his influence.

I fell under that influence early, as did George, and we found as fledgling writers that we couldn't have had a better mentor and guide to what was best and most important about SF.

So it seems appropriate to end this group of interviews with James Gunn, who has described his mission as "saving the world through science fiction" and who has done more than almost anyone else to keep SF alive and relevant as a literature.

—Pamela Sargent
Albany, New York
May 1, 2018

York City on May 12, 2007, where Jim Gunn was honored with the Grand Master Award.

ISAAC ASIMOV:
The Last Interview

George Zebrowski: I'd like to ask you what your deepest feelings were when you first started to write. What did you wish for most from the effort? How did you imagine it would be?

Isaac Asimov: When I first started to write (at the age of eleven) I had only the feeling that I wanted to write. I didn't know why, I just wanted to make up a story.

By the time I was eighteen, I had gotten to a new stage. I wanted to see my story in print, with my name on it. That was all I dreamed of, to see my name in *Astounding*. The thought of money never entered into it. Seeing my name was great—all I thought it would be, and when money arrived *also*, it turned out to be welcome because I needed money for college.

After that it was just a matter of trying to do better—and better—

Zebrowski: Was it true that behind this initial desire to see your work in print there existed a deep love of the science fiction you read in boyhood and the impulse to add to its beauties with work of your own? And could you tell us which works of the 1930s most impressed you?

Asimov: Yes, I was an ardent reader of science fiction from the age of nine. From 1929 to 1938 I read every scrap of science fiction I could lay my hands on. As for my favorite stories of the period, they appear in my anthology *Before the Golden Age*.

Among the novels I particularly loved were Jack Williamson's *The Legion of Space* and *The Cometeers*, all of E. E. Smith, particularly *Galactic Patrol*, Edmond Hamilton's *The Universe Wreckers*.

Once I started publishing science fiction it became more of a business for me and I could no longer love it with the wild abandon of my younger days—perhaps because that kind of wild abandon is only to be found in younger days.

Zebrowski: Which of your own works do you like most? Could you answer this in each category—short fiction, novels, and especially nonfiction?

Asimov: Short fiction: My favorite story is "The Last Question," which was first published in *Science Fiction Quarterly* in 1956.

Novels: My favorite novel is *The Gods Themselves*, published by Doubleday in 1972. It won the Hugo and the Nebula but that's not why it's my favorite.

Nonfiction: My favorite nonfiction books are my various autobiographies: *In Memory Yet Green* (Doubleday, 1979); *In Joy Still Felt* (Doubleday, 1980), and one that is forthcoming.[3]

Zebrowski: Why, then, is *The Gods Themselves* your favorite novel?

Asimov: Because when I reread it (as I did recently) I cannot help but notice that I was writing over my head, especially in the second part. It seemed to me that my writing was better and more skillful than usual. Just luck, I suppose, for I don't remember working on it any differently from the way I worked on my other novels.

I admit that in the second part I was meeting a "dare." Because I avoid sex in my novels and extraterrestrials, I have heard it said that I couldn't handle either. I was determined to show those who said so that they were quite wrong. In the second part I dealt with extraterrestrials that were *really* different, and it dealt only with sex. Every time I think of the book I think with satisfaction of having showed those who underestimated me that they shouldn't.

Zebrowski: Many of my colleagues share my opinion that *The Gods Themselves* is one of your best works, because it is modern in technique, filled with original ideas and touches provocatively on issues of science and government. We also include *The Caves of Steel*, *The Naked Sun*, *The End of Eternity*, and in short fiction "The Dead Past," "The Ugly Little Boy," and "The Martian Way." The author of these works speaks in a gracefully lucid and sophisticated voice. Yet you have on various occasions, most recently in your Author's Note to your new novel, *Nemesis*, renounced "art-

3   Doubleday published the third volume, *I, Asimov: A Memoir*, in 1994.

istry," so-called. I say so-called, because I don't believe you to be against genuine artistry, but only against the pretentious kind. It seems to me that the writer whose works Anthony Burgess has described as "no easy fripperies for a loose-end evening; they demand concentration as Henry James demands it" has been unfair to his own accomplishments.

Asimov: I renounce any claim to "artistry" simply because I don't sweat over my books. I write them as quickly as I can and I never look back. I don't polish and I don't revise except where necessary to correct actual errors. In order to do this, I deliberately write in as simple and straightforward a manner as possible, eschewing all fanciness.

Maybe what I mean by "artistry" is "fanciness." Maybe there is art to plain writing, but if there is, I put it in on the unconscious level—never deliberately.

I have been accused by critics of having "no style," but I pay no attention to that. What they mean is no "fanciness," and that's very true. The only difference is that they think I ought to have some and I don't.

Zebrowski: I'd like to widen our discussion, if I may. In a recent editorial in *Asimov's*, you expressed astonishment that Robert A. Heinlein could have had so much trouble with editors and publishers during his career. I'd like to ask you why you were astonished. As an observer of the publishing scene for many years, surely you've noticed that the regard in which a writer is held doesn't always carry over to how an editor or publisher treats that writer. Greg Bear has observed that SF tends to eat and spit out many of its best. What did you think of the issues I raised in my review of Heinlein's letters, *Grumbles from the Grave*?

Asimov: Since this is Rosh Hashanah (the Jewish New Year) let me quote a story from the Bible. You will find it in 2 Chronicles 1: 7-12:

> In that night did God appear unto Solomon, and said unto him, Ask what I shall give thee. And Solomon said unto God…Give me now wisdom and knowledge, that I may go out and come in before this people: for who can judge this thy people, that is so great.

And God said to Solomon, Because this was in thine heart, and thou hast not asked riches, wealth, or honor, nor the life of thine enemies, neither yet has asked long life; but has asked wisdom and knowledge for thyself, that thou mayest judge my people…

Wisdom and knowledge is granted unto thee; and I will give thee riches, and wealth, and honor…

Well, the following did *not* happen but if it could have happened, this is what would have happened:

Fifty years ago God appeared to me and said, Ask what I shall give thee. And Isaac said to God…Give me now the desire to write and the gift of being published. It is all I want.

And God said to Isaac, Because this was in your heart, and you have not asked for riches, wealth, or honor, or large advances, or great promotion, or long life, the desire to write and the gift of being published is granted to you, and I will give you riches, and wealth, and honor, and large advances, and promotion and long life.

And that's it, George. I have made a deal with every publisher I have, especially Doubleday, and it is just this. They publish everything I give them to publish, and I won't ask for any large advances—or any advance at all if necessary—or ask questions about sales—or make demands about promotion—or want special treatment.

And, as a result, Doubleday has published 113 of my books, including large numbers of books of essays, and annotations of the Bible, of Shakespeare, of Gilbert and Sullivan, and so on. They have never rejected a book (except once, come to think of it, to their regret) and have never seriously fooled around with anything I have written. And they give me advances that are larger than I want and they recycle and reprint my books endlessly and treat me always as a favored child—and all because I don't ask for anything but publication.

This holds true for my other publishers, too. One of them said to me once, "You're our best author, but what is amazing is that you're our nicest author, too. Those two things never go together."

So it was a great discovery that I made, and I'm not selfish. I give it to all of you freely. Nice guys finish first.

As for Robert Heinlein, there is no question but that he was more highly regarded than I as a science fiction writer (*only* as a science fiction writer) and undoubtedly made more money than I did, but no one can read *Grumbles* without seeing that he was an unhappy man, while no one can read my two-volume autobiography without seeing that I was a happy one.

Bob was unhappy because he had a highly developed sense of being cheated by every editor he dealt with, and I suspect that most writers feel the same way (with varying degrees of justification for all I know). I have no such sense. I always assume an editor is on my side. If I make money, he makes money and vice versa, and as far as I know, this has worked.

Your description of Heinlein in your review of *Grumbles* I don't recognize except for his suggestion that you support Jeane Kirkpatrick for vice president in 1988. She would make even Quayle look good.

It is possible that this answer may be used as "evidence" that I have a colossal ego, but the hell with it. I'm too old and too secure to give a damn what anyone says.

Zebrowski: Which SF writers of recent decades, say since 1965, have you found worthy or enjoyable? Which writers have you disliked? Or, more generally, what trends in SF have you disapproved of?

Asimov: Forgive me, George, but it is impossible for me to answer the first part of this question. I don't like to judge my colleagues; first, because it isn't fair, and, second, because I don't consider myself qualified to do so.

A trend in science fiction that I disapprove of is the increasing tendency to write Tolkien imitations. None of them are within a light-year of Tolkien, and they squeeze *real* science fiction into a narrower compass.

Zebrowski: What nonfictional scientific works have you admired over the years?

Asimov: I was very fond of *The Making of the Atomic Bomb* by [Richard] Rhodes. I also go for any book on science by Martin Gardner, L. Sprague de Camp, Stephen Jay Gould, Paul Davis, or Timothy Ferris.

Zebrowski: Which works of fiction, not SF, have you admired over the years?

Asimov: I'm a great reader of Charles Dickens, Mark Twain, P.G. Wodehouse, and Agatha Christie. I've read everything they've written over and over again, and I don't intend ever to stop rereading them.

Zebrowski: Your new novel, *Nemesis*, is your first book in some time that does not belong to a series. What moved you to write it?

Asimov: I was moved to write it by my Doubleday editor, Jennifer Brehl, who *ordered* me to write a book that was not part of any series. So I did, just to show her that I could.

Zebrowski: What are you working on now? What other works of fiction do you have planned? Is there a book entitled *Foundation and Eternity* somewhere ahead?

Asimov: The novel I am working on now is *Forward the Foundation*. Again, its details are following an order by Jennifer Brehl. She wanted a Foundation novel, which, like the first three, was not unitary. For that reason I said that I would write it as five interconnected novellas. I have completed two and am working on the third. It is very hard to do—five separate plots, which advance the overall plot. One of these years I've got to stop accepting challenges just to show off.

Zebrowski: As a final question to this interview, what would you have liked for me to ask that I did not?

Asimov: I don't think you have asked me if I have had a happy life as a writer. The answer is:

You betcha.

I'm approaching the end of my life now, but as I look back on it, it has been filled with the excitement and drama and satisfaction of writing. I have done almost nothing else—haven't traveled, haven't had parties, haven't had "fun"—just sat at the typewriter and worked.

Do I regret it now?

Never.

All I have is this vague feeling that I would like to start all over again and this time write *more* and on *more* different subjects. I regret the small bits of my life in which I didn't write and which I wasted.

An Interview with
RAY BRADBURY

George Zebrowski: Let's start with an uneasy question. Ray, what were your feelings when you started writing? What did you hope for?

Ray Bradbury: Hah! I just wanted to be a good writer, that's all. I was twelve years old.

Zebrowski: That early?

Bradbury: Sure.

Zebrowski: You had what seems to have been a long apprenticeship—from the late 1930s to the early 1950s. Why do you think it took a long while, as it does for so many writers? Did it seem long to you?

Bradbury: No. Every day was wonderful. You just do it because you love it. I wrote a lot of good short stories all through the '40s. I began to be a good writer when I was 22, that's in 1942, so it didn't take as long as it looks. Took about ten years.

Zebrowski: Now when you, arrived, so to speak, with *The Martian Chronicles* (Doubleday, 1950), you did so not only in the world of science fiction and fantasy but also in the world of American letters. Did this surprise you?

Bradbury: It didn't happen just then—I didn't arrive anywhere. The book didn't sell worth a damn. It didn't get any reviews. One review by Christopher Isherwood. It sold five thousand copies. So I didn't exactly arrive.

Zebrowski: Well, by the time I got to it in the late '50s, it certainly seemed that way to me.

Bradbury: Well, you were a member of a minority—a few thousand people.

Zebrowski: Now whose idea was it to make a book of the Martian stories? Was it your own?

Bradbury: No, it was Walter Bradbury, the editor of Doubleday. I had dinner with him when I went there in 1949. My wife was pregnant, we had no money. I went to New York to meet the editors, and they all said, don't you have a novel? I said no, I have short stories. At dinner one night with Walter Bradbury, no relation to me, he said, "What about all those Martian stories? If you tied them together in a tapestry, wouldn't they make a book called *The Martian Chronicles*?" I said, "Oh, my God!" So he said, "Write me an outline, and give it to me tomorrow at the editorial offices, and if I like it I'll give you seven hundred and fifty dollars." So I stayed up all night and wrote an outline, and he gave me an advance the next day.

Zebrowski: And how did you feel?

Bradbury: I felt fine. I was rich, suddenly.

Zebrowski: Yes, well, it was much more money back then. Would you tell me something about your association with John Huston and the scripting of *Moby Dick*? It always seemed to me that you were the perfect choice to write the script. When I saw your name on the screen, I said, "Of course!"

Bradbury: It was very difficult. He was a strange man. He could be wonderful, he could be a monster. He didn't know anything about *Moby Dick*, so he couldn't really help me. The main thing was he egged me on, and so I finally got the script finished. But it was a strange relationship, and I'm very grateful for it, of course, because it was my first screenplay.

Zebrowski: You've often talked about preventing futures rather than predicting or advocating them. Do you see good science fiction as a kind of cultural vaccine against evil futures?

Bradbury: Oh it can be. I mean *Fahrenheit 451* is a perfect example of wrong things I wrote about that have come to pass, and we're living through them right now. Trying to make do with lousy TV. Dreadful TV news. The news on every station in America today, local TV news, is an abomination. You mustn't look at it, you mustn't listen to it. It's all lies. It's all building up things that shouldn't be built up. There's no real news. It's all fifteen-second sound bites. It's all violence, it's all murder, it's all rape. There is no news.

Zebrowski: It's all to sell products. Now do you think, however, that science fiction should strive to depict desirable futures, or is that impossible or undesirable?

Bradbury: No, you shouldn't strive to do anything. Just do your work and if it's positive, fine, and if it's negative, fine. Whoever you are, whatever you need to write—do your work, and then if it influences people, swell, but you can't set out to do that.

Zebrowski: Then you've never tried to imagine a desirable future?

Bradbury: No.

Zebrowski: Could you describe one? Would that be possible?

Bradbury: No, I don't think so. If it happens in a story, swell. There are good and bad things in the culture, constantly. The automobile is a wonderful device and a horrible device. It can transport us, it can change civilizations, and it has killed two million people so far.

Zebrowski: But there are innovations that could be desirable?

Bradbury: Well, the rocket ship is one. Space travel is one of the most beautiful things that has ever happened to mankind.

Zebrowski: Tell me, what writers do you most admire?

Bradbury: Jules Verne, H. G. Wells, F. Scott Fitzgerald, early John Steinbeck, the short stories of Hemingway, Eudora Welty, Katherine Anne Porter, Jessamyn West…

Zebrowski: What do you most admire about Hemingway?"

Bradbury: Let's talk about a real writer—John Collier. One of the most important writers of the twentieth century, yet most people don't know his name.

Zebrowski: Sadly, that's so.

Bradbury: He had a true imagination, he had a gift of metaphor, and he was a great influence on me.

Zebrowski: Aside from writers, what people have you admired during your long career?

Bradbury: Well, people like Federico Fellini, the film director. Loren Eiseley, who headed the department of anthropology at the University of Pennsylvania. His essays on anthropology were a great influence on me all through my late twenties and thirties. I wrote him a fan letter and encouraged him to write a book back around 1948. He responded and said, "By God, I think that's a good idea." He set out and wrote thirty books, so I'm glad to say I was an influence on his life.

Zebrowski: Yes, and I've often linked him with your work in my mind.

Bradbury: Wonderful, wonderful man.

Zebrowski: When last we talked, you mentioned the help you received from Robert Heinlein, from Leigh Brackett, and from Henry Kuttner. What was your experience with these notable writers?

Bradbury: Well, especially with Leigh Brackett. I met her at the beach every Sunday afternoon from the time I was twenty-one to the time I was twenty-five, and we'd sit on the beach and I'd read her wonderful short stories and she'd read my terrible ones. And I hadn't learned to write yet, and she put up with this garbage that I was writing. I wrote imitations of her stories, and finally I broke free and began to write stuff from my own psyche, and by the time I was twenty-five I was beginning to write some good stuff; but it was meeting with her every Sunday, watching her play volleyball and reading her short stories that helped me. Later in this period she married Edmond Hamilton, and the couple were influences on me. I was best man at their wedding. Edmond was a beautifully educated man, and he introduced me to some of the greatest writers in the world. So I was lucky to have them as friends. Henry Kuttner was a constant critic. I can't say we were close friends, but we were close critical friends. He read my short stories and kicked me around the block when I needed it. I have dozens of letters from him, from my early twenties. He tried to sell my short stories for me. He contacted John W. Campbell, but he didn't get anywhere selling me to Campbell. He in turn sold Campbell a lot of wonderful fiction. I was privileged to know Kuttner as a casual friend.

Zebrowski: And Robert Heinlein?

Bradbury: No, I didn't really know Heinlein that well. I met him when I was nineteen, and he was thirty-one. He had just sold his first short stories. He joined the Science Fiction League in L.A., and I would see him on occasion. He sold my first short story for me. He sent it to Rob Wagner's *Script*. It was my first appearance in print. I was twenty years old, and I was very much beholden to Heinlein for that act of kindness.

Zebrowski: Was it Kuttner who sent you his manuscripts after he was finished with them?

Bradbury: He gave me a lot of his typescripts, yes.

Zebrowski: In advising young writers, you suggest that they not read their contemporaries, but stick with Shakespeare, Pope, Pepys...

Bradbury: That's for later. You gotta read your contemporaries when you're nineteen years old to know what's going on. But as you get older you should break free—don't go on reading in science fiction and fantasy, because you're going to imitate, repeat the clichés. The trouble with science fiction today is that you see all these repetitions of titles and themes that are repeats of other themes—galactic empires, dungeons and dragons. That's terrible. You have to break free from that.

Zebrowski: Who are the greatest writers that you like to read?

Bradbury: F. Scott Fitzgerald. I go to Paris every July and I take a copy of *Tender Is the Night* and I sit in outdoor restaurants and drink coffee and have a beer and I read the novel.

Zebrowski: What are you working on now, Ray?

Bradbury: Three novels, two books of short stories, a book of poetry, and two books of essays. Outside of that, nothing.

Zebrowski: Are the essays previously published?

Bradbury: Some are, from various magazines. I have an article coming in *National Geographic*.

Zebrowski: And you have a story reprinted in *Skylife*,[4] edited by Gregory Benford and George Zebrowski.

Bradbury: That's right!

Zebrowski: We're very glad to have you in the collection. What are you reading now?

Bradbury: I'm rereading George Bernard Shaw, and Shakespeare, and Alexander Pope. There are not many living writers worth bothering with. I go back and reread Steinbeck and Hemingway, and books of essays by Aldous Huxley. I'm so busy writing, though, that I don't have much time to read.

Zebrowski: I know the problem. What changes do you see in the publishing industry since you started?

Bradbury: Well, it's easier to become a science fiction writer. There are hundreds of books a year published in science fiction and fantasy. When I was growing up and trying to become a writer, there were seven or eight books a year. So there are more opportunities open to the young writer.

4   This anthology was published in 2000 by Houghton Mifflin Harcourt.

Zebrowski: And what changes for better or worse do you see in the science fiction and fantasy fields?

Bradbury: I can only guess, since I don't read in the field. I can't judge.

Zebrowski: Let me ask you, is there a question that you would have liked me to ask, and if so, what is it?

Bradbury: Well, you might have asked me if I will ever write an opera, and the answer is yes. I've written several musicals, I've written a dramatic semi-opera for *Fahrenheit 451*, which was performed in Chicago and in New York, and will have performances all around the world in the next year. I'm working on a grand opera called *Leviathan 99*, which is based on a play of mine about Moby Dick in outer space—the Great White Comet. I've taken the metaphors and transferred them from sailing ships to rocket ships, from the open seas of the world to the open seas of stars and space, and Ahab is the space captain whose eyes have been put out by a comet when he was a young astronaut, and he goes out into the universe seeking this great white comet, which he seeks to destroy. This is the subject matter of my opera, which I hope will be written with Jerry Goldsmith, the composer.

Zebrowski: The film composer.

Bradbury: He's one of the best.

Zebrowski: Films have been made of your work. Generally, how have you found them?

Bradbury: Well, I love *Something Wicked This Way Comes.* It's not perfect, but it's damn good. *Fahrenheit 451* is quite good, except they left out a lot of things. I'm hoping that if it's filmed by Mel Gibson that he'll put a lot of things back. But I'm not very optimistic because years have gone by and he never calls. So I don't know what's gonna happen next.[5]

Zebrowski: Well, it seems that you're as busy as ever.

Bradbury: I'll be eighty in August.

Zebrowski: Only eighty. Well, you and Charles L. Harness and Jack Williamson. Well, Jack Williamson makes you all look young.

Bradbury: Jack is a wonderful man, a terrific man. He was very kind to me when I was nineteen years old. He read my stuff

---

5   A new adaptation of *Fahrenheit 451* was shown on HBO in the spring of 2018.

long before Leigh Brackett did, and it was really bad in those days.

Zebrowski: It's hard for me to think that Frederik Pohl read Jack Williamson when Fred was eleven.

Bradbury: Jack started publishing in magazines when I was about seven or eight years old.

Zebrowski: Incredible.

Bradbury: I couldn't afford to buy the magazines, but I borrowed copies from friends on occasion, and I read Jack Williamson first.

Zebrowski: Well, I thank you for your snappy answers to my questions.

Bradbury: Well, I'm wide awake, I had my nap!

Zebrowski: Thank you, Ray. I'm honored.

An Interview with
ARTHUR C. CLARKE

George Zebrowski: In your introduction to the 1984 edition of *Profiles of the Future* you wrote: "I also believe—and hope—that politics and economics will cease to be as important in the future as they have been in the past; the time will come when most of our present controversies on these matters will seem as trivial, or as meaningless, as the theological debates in which the keenest minds of the Middle Ages dissipated their energies. Politics and economics are concerned with power and wealth, neither of which should be the primary, still less the exclusive concern of full-grown men."

Given this view, would you describe politics, especially, as a pathology, whose power struggles should be identified as such and then rejected?

Arthur C. Clarke: My crack at economics and politics was, of course, rather tongue-in-cheek. I'm afraid that these are unavoidable necessities in almost any society one can imagine. As I'm speaking, at the height, or depth, of the Clinton Caper, I am tempted to say that politics is a pathology, at least as practiced in the US of A at the moment. But nobody is in the position of throwing stones at anybody else.

Zebrowski: But given that this is the way issues are dealt with in our world, how might politics be replaced?

Clarke: I can only hope that improved education and communication, which will enable us to appreciate, if not share, other countries' and societies' points of view, will make politics healthier. And there is only one way of resolving political disputes. As Winston Churchill said many years ago, "Democracy is the worst form of government, except for all the others."

Zebrowski: With economics, might not one ask that even if technology gives us a world without scarcity, will not people still struggle for power?

Clarke: Technology can certainly give us a world without scarcity. Another famous figure's quote: "There's enough for everyone's need, but not enough for everyone's greed." (Gandhi) People will always struggle for power, and this isn't necessarily a bad thing.

Zebrowski: But how will we overcome our problems if we do not first achieve self-mastery? How would we achieve the self-mastery that would make politics and economics less oppressive to mature human beings? How do we get to this maturity?

Clarke: The world would be a very dull place if there was no personal interaction and even competition. What matters are the methods employed. And contrary to the Declaration of Independence, we aren't born equal. See J. B. S. Haldane's collection of essays, *The Inequality of Man* (London, 1932). I'm rather fond of a cartoon, probably in *The New Yorker*, showing a psychiatrist telling his patient, "You don't have an inferiority complex. You're just inferior."

Zebrowski: Turning to other matters, in a recent front page article on global warming, *The New York Times* asked whether the uncertainties in the science justify inaction?

Clarke: This is obviously a major concern. My friend, Professor Fred Singer, who we British space cadets brainwashed into joining us in the late '40s, has written a book doubting the whole thing. We need more information, but there are obviously things that should be done, whatever the final verdict. For example, the avoidance of unnecessary pollution. But if in fact, as some people believe, this is the end of the current inter-glacial period, we may be encouraged to burn fossil fuels to build up the carbon dioxide content to create global warming to keep the glaciers at bay. Many years ago I wrote a story called "The Forgotten Enemy," in which I had the glaciers coming back within a few years. Sharmini Tiruchelvan thought that was very unscientific, but now there is evidence that the climate flip-over can indeed occur in a few decades, not millennia.

Zebrowski: But what is your opinion of the continued warming of Alaska, where for the first time the permafrost is melting and large areas are falling into sinkholes?

(The phone rang at this point.) A little later...

Clarke: ...I had to stop dictation to receive a phone call from a woman who was once called the most beautiful in the world. I have her portrait by [Pietro] Annigoni, or at least a copy of it, hanging on my wall. She is also a concert pianist, and has written books on cookery, and is now working on a novel. It doesn't seem fair that people have so many talents, does it?

Zebrowski: Moving to a more personal note, would you talk about people you have admired or looked up to?

Clarke: People I've admired or looked up to...if I restrict myself to people I've actually met or known, and delete historical characters, like Newton or Shakespeare...um, proceeding more or less at random, um...Lord Dunsany, who I met only once—and I've written quite a bit about him. In fact our correspondence has been published now. Olaf Stapledon—very much so, of course he made a colossal influence on me. I only met him a couple of times. J. B. S. Haldane. John R. Pierce and Harold Rosen, the true fathers of the communications satellite. And of course Stanley Kubrick. I've written a whole book about our encounters, the result of which is widely known. See *The Lost Worlds of 2001*.

I have so many friends in the science fiction and science fields, it's very hard to place one above others. But I've always had a special feeling for Ray Bradbury, Robert Bloch, and E. E. Smith, who I only met once, and consider to be a much underrated writer.

Zebrowski: Perhaps we can return to this subject a little later. In the meantime, I'd like to ask you my favorite question. What did you feel when you first started to write fiction? How did you envision the effort? What did you hope for?

Clarke: That's nearly seventy years ago, and I haven't the faintest idea.

It was just fun, I'm sure. I never imagined I'd be able to make a living out of it. And of course it did begin as an amateur occupation, in the various fan magazines. All I hoped for at the time is that it would be enjoyed by my friends. And later on, as I got involved with The British Interplanetary Society and the space movement generally, I realized I could use fiction to put across my ideas, not just purely for entertainment. Though I'm always fond of quoting Sam Goldwyn's now outdated, "If you gotta message, use Western Union." I suppose he'd say today, email or the web.

Zebrowski: How do you feel about your fiction today?

Clarke: Well, I haven't looked at it for years. In fact I can scarcely ever remember rereading any of my fiction. Writing has always been a sort of hole in my life, and perhaps I resent the fact that it was a way to avoid living—although of course it has enabled me to live as I wished to do.

Zebrowski: How do you feel about your nonfiction?

Clarke: I have been rereading that for *Greetings, Carbon-Based Bipeds!*, which Ian T. Macauley is editing for St. Martin's Press, for publication in August, 1999. I've seldom drawn the distinction between my nonfiction and fiction writing, although of course I've made it quite clear in the context—but they've been the opposite sides of the same coin, with many themes and ideas, concepts in both fiction and nonfiction, starting on one side and moving to the other. Perhaps the best example is an essay I was asked to write about the star of Bethlehem, which eventually led to the short story, "The Star."

Zebrowski: Which won the 1956 Hugo Award for Best Short Story, after being rejected by the major slicks. As noted by your biographer, Neil McAleer, "The Star" was considered "blasphemous" by *The Saturday Evening Post*. I recall that even many years later, the television adaptation for the new Twilight Zone series was watered down to be more acceptable. The story appeared in one of the lesser science fiction magazines of 1955, *Infinity Science Fiction.*

Clarke: I'd like to revert to your earlier question of people I've looked up to or admired...there must be so many in my lifetime that it's hard to do justice to them all. But what I'm doing, cunningly, is going through the index of the Arthur C. Clarke biography you mentioned—an amazing book. I don't know how McAleer gathered all that information. I'll note the people who have influenced me. Here they are, and not necessarily in alphabetical order.

Four people I enormously admire, because of their connection with the conquest of space:

James Webb, who was NASA's administrator after deputy administrator Hugh L. Dryden. Webb is now almost a forgotten man, but I don't think the Apollo Program would have succeeded without his drive. Then Thomas O. Paine, who was NASA's administrator after Webb. And of course Wernher von Braun, the driving force behind the development of the giant Saturn rocket. Wernher was the one I knew best. I'd known him for many years, and I'm sorry that now there's a sort of campaign against him because of his association with the Nazis, who he thoroughly disliked. This raises a moral issue. Of course, the atomic scientists were also being criticized. I'm not going to come down on either side of this difficult argument.

Webb, Paine, and von Braun are all dead, but somebody who happily is not is George E. Mueller. He is NASA's associate director of Manned Space Flight, and a very good friend.

I admire these men for their ability to accept responsibility on an enormous scale, something I don't think I could ever do. In fact one of my aims has always been "Power without Responsibility," and as a writer I think I've probably achieved that.

Continuing through my list of names, Walter Cronkite is a man I've always admired, since we started working together in the 1960s, I think, when I joined him and Wally Schirra on the Apollo coverage. Walter is, I think, exactly as he appears to be, a real thoroughly nice man. I've had the pleasure of showing him around Sri Lanka and taking him for a ride in my hovercraft. He once took me for a trip in his sailboat, off Martha's Vineyard, and when we got back to land I said, "Walter, I now understand the feelings of the man who said why should you go to all this trouble when you can get exactly the same sensation by standing in a cold shower and tearing up hundred dollar bills." Today, thousand dollar bills! I was happy to meet him in the Hotel Chelsea in October of 1999—he hasn't changed a bit!

Another man I liked and admired, and who died at a tragically early age, and is now almost forgotten, was the British writer John Keir Cross, who wrote a number of science fiction and fantasy stories in the '40s and '50s, and did a lot of radio plays, and also adapted some science fiction for radio. He was the first, I think, professional writer I got to know. He lived not far from me when I moved to north London, and he had quite an influence on me, and encouraged me, I think, to become a pro.

And talking of pros, of course, my late and sadly missed Isaac Asimov is the epitome, although the pro of pros is Robert Silverberg. Isaac and I had a long relationship—and of course you know about our comic feud.

Zebrowski: You're referring, of course, to the famous Clarke-

Asimov Treaty, about which Isaac has written in *I, Asimov: A Memoir* (Doubleday, 1994): "We came to an agreement many years ago in a taxi which, at the time, was moving south on Park Avenue, so it is called the Treaty of Park Avenue. By it, I have agreed to maintain, on questioning, that Arthur is the best science fiction writer in the world, though I am allowed to say, if questioned assiduously, that I am breathing down his neck as we run. In return, Arthur has agreed to insist, forever, that I am the best science writer in the world. He must say it, whether he believes it or not."

Clarke: We always needled each other. Some people probably thought it was for real, but I don't think either of us had the slightest jealousy of the other's success. We only pretended to.

Continuing through my list of names, another writer I admire greatly was John Brunner, who I think was perhaps the most brilliant of all the British science fiction writers, and never achieved the success he should have done. He died at a tragically early age, of a heart attack at the World Science Fiction Convention in Glasgow, 1995.

Zebrowski: Brunner was in many ways a beloved figure, but at the time of his death nearly all his books were out of print in Britain and the United States.

* * * *

Clarke: Carl Sagan has recorded how I started his career as a writer and science popularizer. The essay I wrote about him in Roddy McDowell's *Double Exposure* (Third Edition) describes our relationship. Incidentally, I was very sad that Roddy died recently. I met him here in Sri Lanka briefly, and he was a very nice, sweet person, best remembered, I expect, for his Planet of the Apes appearances.

Gene Roddenberry is another person I admired, and I was able to help in his early struggles when the studios didn't think Star Trek had any potential. He's described our relationship in the biography that Yvonne Fern has written about him (*Gene Roddenberry: The Last Conversation*).

I can't fail to mention Roger Caras, whom I met first when he was Stanley Kubrick's Vice President on *2001*.[6] Roger has had

---

6   Roger Caras was an assistant and publicist for *2001: A Space Odyssey*.

many careers now, among them president of the American Society for the Prevention of Cruelty to Animals. He's done a lot of radio and television about animal welfare. He's quite a character.

And while we're on Hollywood, dear old George Pal, who made some of the best early science fiction movies. I only met him a couple of times, and he invited me on the set when he was filming *The War of the Worlds* (1953), and I saw one of the Martian explosions being done by one of the special effects people. They wouldn't do that sort of thing nowadays, with so much secrecy surrounding everything.

Another friend from my early radio and TV days was Olga Druce, who produced the Captain Video series, which incredibly were done in real time, five nights a week. No videotape then!

Zebrowski: And just as incredible today is the fact that only one episode of this series survives in kinescope.

Clarke: Olga was a dear friend, and tried to get me involved in Captain Video. I was wise enough not to accept, but that didn't affect our friendship.

Zebrowski: One of your own stories, "All The Time in the World," survives handsomely from this period, as adapted on *Tales of Tomorrow*, with teleplay by one Arthur C. Clark (name misspelled in the credits). It reruns often on the Sci-Fi Channel.

Clarke: You must send me a copy. I wonder if I'm due any royalties.

Zebrowski: I will.

Clarke: Moving on. Hugo Gernsback. How could I have forgotten him?

I think we only met once. Dinner somewhere. Of course, he's rather a controversial character. His reluctance to pay his authors may have been involuntary, but he certainly had a tremendous impact on the field.

The Hugo Award is justly named after him. We did have one comic encounter some years later. He wrote, chastising me for saying that the Orbital Post Office had been invented by me. He claimed to have thought of it first. I was able to reply that it had appeared (1) before he'd said he invented it, in a book of mine, which (2) was dedicated to him! I had a very amusing, contrite reply.

Ian and Betty Ballantine, of course, had a great influence on me. They accepted my early novels, and I was happy to get a

Christmas card from Betty only the other day. (Just phoned 80th b'day greetings!) Their impact on the science fiction field was enormous, matched only perhaps by that of Judy-Lynn del Rey and her husband Lester del Rey. There's a photograph, I believe in *Locus*, of my then agent, the late Scott Meredith, and Judy, who came down to Washington to sign the contract for my next two novels. I think they were *2010: Odyssey Two* and *The Songs of Distant Earth*. When Judy passed me the advances of one dollar and ten cents, I passed the ten cents and one penny on to Scott for his commission. Incidentally, I think I can claim to have received the lowest rate of payment any author has or had or will receive [laughs], for a one page story that Frederik Pohl published under the title, "A Recursion In Metastories," in the October 1966 *Galaxy* magazine. My title had been "The Longest Science-Fiction Story Ever Told." Fred wrote in his editorial note, "Clever of us to get it on a single page!" It contains an infinite number of words.

Zebrowski: I recall that there was an illustration by Jack Gaughan on the facing page. Does that make it two pages?

* * * *

Clarke: One of the people I most admired, and met quite a number of times, was Buckminster Fuller. I had the privilege of flying him around Sri Lanka once, and contributing a plug to his final volumes, *Synergetics* and *Synergetics 2*. What a pity that he never lived to see the discovery of the Buckminster Fullerene molecule, which will make possible the space elevator one day, as depicted in *The Fountains of Paradise*.

Zebrowski: I was particularly gratified by the Fullerine's discovery, because it was fashionable in the '60s, when I was in college, to denigrate Fuller, especially in philosophy circles, and here was nature imitating a great thinker's insight.

* * * *

Clarke: Another person who had a great but indirect influence on my life was Jacques-Yves Cousteau, the co-inventor of the aqualung. We met a couple of times, and more recently I met his son. Cousteau was a great man, and a great popularizer of the ocean and its inhabitants.

Again, as in the case of von Braun, there's a reaction against his reputation now.

Another important influence on my life, of course, has been Gentry Lee, who was introduced to me by Peter Guber, who wanted to make a film based on Gentry's ideas. It was never filmed, but it led to the novel *Cradle*, which was based on our joint ideas but almost entirely written by Gentry. Since then Gentry has collaborated on *Rama II* and *The Garden of Rama*, and *Rama Revealed*, which was written virtually entirely by him, though with consultation with me. I've described our collaboration in the preface, "Co-Authors and Other Nuisances," I think in *Rama II*.

My mind seems to be slipping into the past, so I'd like to give a tribute to my first editor, Walter Gillings, one of the pioneers of science fiction in England during, good heavens—the 1930s. Wally, to whom I dedicated my first collection, *Expedition to Earth* (1953), gave me my very first typewriter, a massive vertical machine, which will now be a valuable antique. I think it's still in the Clarkives. I remember carrying it back in a London bus, and I tapped out my first stories on that machine. Walter launched the first British science fiction magazine, *Science Fantasy*, in 1950, and was a very dear friend. Like Ted Carnell, another of the early science fiction pioneers.

Another writer who influenced me very much was Eric Frank Russell. I don't know how well he's remembered now, but he was the first of us to break through into the American *Unknown Worlds*, John W. Campbell's companion magazine to *Astounding*, with his novel, *Sinister Barrier*, in 1939. He wrote many excellent stories, which are I'm sure well worth reading. I seem to recall that my very first money from fiction was as a result of giving some ideas to Eric, which he duly incorporated in one of his stories. Don't ask me which one.

Zebrowski: No problem. The story is "The Prr-r-eet," and was inspired by Stanley Weinbaum's "A Martian Odyssey." It was published in *Tales of Wonder*, edited by Walter H. Gillings on June 29, 1937. Sam Moskowitz's *Seekers of Tomorrow* (1966) records that the alien being of the title gives humankind "a device for simultaneously blending color and sound into a new type of music. This idea was supplied by Arthur C. Clarke, who had met Russell at a London meeting of the Science Fiction Association, and he received 10 percent of the proceeds for his contribution, something under three dollars, but was the first money Clarke ever earned from science fiction."

Clarke: Another writer that I knew very well was John Benyon Harris, better known as John Wyndham, whose 1951 *The Day of the Triffids* seems an immortal story. It's often being revived in some form or another. John was a very nice guy, but unfortunately suffered from an almost fatal defect for a fiction writer: he had a private income. If he hadn't, I'm sure he'd have written much more.

I seem to be traveling further and further back in time, but I'd be remiss if I didn't give a tribute to my very first schoolmaster, Arnold Goodliffe at Huish's Grammar School. He was an impressive man in the best Dr. Arnold tradition, and I think filled us all with awe. And later still, my English master, a fiery Welshman, E. B. Mitford, inspired my early writings for the school magazine. Some of them were published recently in a small collection, a small edition.

I mentioned the influence of E. E. Smith, yet earlier, Edgar Rice Burroughs had probably an even greater influence. And Arthur Conan Doyle, whose *The Lost World* (1912) is still I think a perfect example of the science fiction action story.

I'm sure I could discuss lots of writers from the 30s; yet the one I remember most vividly is still with us, incredibly. I refer of course to the apparently immortal Jack Williamson. I can still recall, it couldn't be later than 1930, passages from *The Green Girl*. I've only met Jack once or twice, if indeed that, but I think he's a superb writer, and deserves much better recognition than he's received.

Zebrowski: I think you'll be happy to know that Haffner Press, a new small house, has just begun a lavish multi-volumed edition of Williamson's work. Volume one, *The Metal Man*, contains the first in hardcovers edition of *The Green Girl*, on permanent paper, thus saving it from the magazine and paperback editions that are rapidly turning to dust. Volume two, *Wolves of Darkness*, is notable for containing the never reprinted novel, *The Stone From the Green Star*, a boyhood favorite of Fred Pohl! *Wizard's Isle* is volume three of a projected eight books, I think.

Clarke: Let me also pay a tribute to the tragically short-lived Stanley Weinbaum. Again, I can recall quite vividly a day in 1934, when "A Martian Odyssey" (*Wonder Stories*, July, 1934) fell into my hands. I think it's the only time that I've ever read a story and had instantly gone back and reread it.

Zebrowski: Are there perhaps one or two books that have had the greatest influence on you?

Clarke: Besides Stapledon's *Last and First Men*, perhaps the book that had the greatest influence on me was David Lasser's *The Conquest of Space* (1931). Until I persuaded my Aunt Nellie to buy me that, having seen it displayed in the window of Smith's Book Store, I had no idea that space travel was for real, or could be one day. It was a great honor to have met David Lasser as a very old man, when he attended a lecture I gave in California. I wish he'd written his memoirs. He got into troubles as a labor organizer in the '30s. He was also assistant editor to Gernsback, I believe, at one time. He told me that one of the grounds on which he was attacked in Congress as a dangerous radical was that he was obviously insane because he had written a book about the possibility of flying to the Moon. As of course did my friend Willy Ley, who was the chief pioneer of space travel in the days before and immediately after the war. I guess Willy was the nearest thing to a polymath I've ever met. His field covered not only astronomy, but also paleontology and most of biology.

Zebrowski: Speaking of space pioneers, I've read that you knew Hermann Oberth.

Clarke: In 1951, when the British Interplanetary Society arranged the second International Congress on Astronautics in London, which I chaired, I had the privilege of having Hermann Oberth as my house guest. He didn't speak much English, and I spoke even less German, but I still have pleasant remembrances of him as a very courteous house guest. It's amazing what he anticipated. Very few things have happened that are not described in his books, although this is even more true of Konstantin Tsiolkovski, the Russian pioneer of astronautics who was half a century earlier than Oberth, and the American, Robert Goddard.

Zebrowski: Speaking of space travel pioneers, you may not recall, but you introduced me to Willy Ley and Wernher von Braun at the American Rocket Society gathering in New York in October of 1961, where I also met you for the first time. It was an incredible evening for a high school student.

Moving along, tell me about Robert A. Heinlein.

Clarke: I must mention Bob Heinlein, who I stayed with on my first visit to America in 1952, at his beautiful house in Colorado Springs, where he and Ginny looked after me very well, and showed me around Pike's Peak and other picturesque places. I later stayed with them when they moved to California, and I am sad that on our final encounter we had a public falling out, which has been well recorded in Neil McAleer's biography of me, and elsewhere.

Zebrowski: What happened?

Clarke: I had rather gate-crashed a meeting at Larry Niven's, at the height of the Star Wars caper, and perhaps tactlessly gave as my whole view that the whole thing was nonsense, which is rather an exaggeration. Clearly there are some things that can and should be done, but from the very beginning I regarded the idea of an umbrella over the entire United States, which some people had been touting, as total technological nonsense. I believe that virtually everyone now agrees with me. The situation then was summed up by my good friend Luis Alvarez, who said that the people behind the more extreme positions were a very bright group with no common sense. How ironic that many years later I had as my house guest in Sri Lanka, George Keyworth and his wife Polly, because it was Jay [Keyworth] as President Reagan's science advisor who actually wrote his notorious Star Wars speech. He had to do, as he said later, a great many drafts in order to retain his credibility with the scientific establishment.

I don't think I mentioned Luis Alvarez earlier. Well, Luis invented the Ground Approach Radar, which was based on his linear radar array, which could produce fantastically narrow beams, a fraction of a degree wide, and I was chosen as RAF technical officer to join the unit, my selection being made by Group Captain Edward Fennessey, who later became director general of British Telecom. Ned later told me that he had selected me because my immediate supervisor had said that "I was quite mad but brilliant." He went on to say that he regarded my selection as one of the best decisions of his career.

I didn't meet Luis Alvarez until well after the war, in fact until I went to California in '53, I imagine. That was before I'd written my novel *Glide Path* (1963), which is a thinly-veiled fictionalization of the Ground Approach Control epic, in that I gave the inventor a Nobel Prize, which I am happy Luis did receive a few years later, for inventing the bubble chamber.

On the last time I met him, Luis told me of an invention he was working on—a pair of binoculars through which you could see the moons of Jupiter and the rings of Saturn. There's no problem getting the necessary magnification, but you can't hold them steady enough to use them. Well, image-stabilizer binoculars have now been produced on exactly the principle Luis was working on. It's an optical system that cancels out the shaking of your hand. I've just bought the SONY 15X magnification pair, and the other night I was able to see three of Jupiter's moons when I switched on the image-stabilizer. I'm sure Luis would have been delighted. End of digressions.

Zebrowski: In *The View from Serendip* (1977), you wrote: "If the decades and the centuries pass with no indication that there is intelligent life in the universe, the long-term effects on human philosophy will be profound, and may be disastrous. Better to have neighbors we don't like than to be utterly alone." How will these effects on the human outlook be profound? How will humanity be affected, one way or the other?

Clarke: In fact I'm now bored to tears with the whole subject of SETI (Search for Extraterrestrial Intelligence), and wish it would have a few decades of benign neglect, especially by the purveyors of mind-rotting garbage in such journals as *The National Prevaricator*.

Still, to have a go at your question. It seems to me that humanity might be overwhelmed by the effect of alien contact. Any intelligent person couldn't fail to be awed by the knowledge that we're not alone in the universe, though of course a great deal depends on what "they," quote-unquote, are like. If they're so superior that we can't begin to comprehend them, the effects might be devastating, as has been seen by the impact on primitive societies by more advanced cultures, even without deliberate attempts at destroying them.

I think it was an American Indian chief who said, "You've stolen our dreams."

We all have to have dreams, and when they are stolen it can be tragic.

Zebrowski: Fermi's Paradox asks, if the universe is so full of life, where are they? What is your answer to Fermi's Paradox, if it is one?

Clarke: I don't have an answer. There are dozens of answers. In no particular order: (1) They know all about us and have sensibly kept away. (2) We're actually quarantined, as C. S. Lewis suggested in *Out of the Silent Planet*. (3) They couldn't care less, or they are so far away they come here every million years or so, and may be back at any moment. (4) Or as I suggested in *2001*, they may be monitoring us, but not doing anything until we become important enough to deserve their attention.

Zebrowski: Everyone has one thing they care most intensely about, we are told. Is there one thing, or more than one, that you care most intensely about?

Clarke: That's an easy one to answer. Melinda, the youngest of the three Ekanayake daughters.[7] And my killer Chihuahua, Pepsi.

Zebrowski: Bertrand Russell once said that at his age he felt that he was humanity, as much as one man can represent it, and that he would speak truthfully about what was most important. If you were addressing humankind, and all its groups were listening, what advice would you give?

Clarke: The best advice I think was given by Douglas Adams: "Don't panic."

And then there was the French general who told his officers: "Above all, not too much zeal."

In other words, avoid fanaticism and intolerance. In fact, intolerance and active cruelty are the two things I hate most.

Zebrowski: In their time, H. G. Wells and Olaf Stapledon scolded humanity. In my view, the world needs to be scolded as Arthur C. Clarke might scold it, as great thinkers and artists have tried to shame it. What would you like to say?

Clarke: I'd hate to be remembered as a scold. You might add Shaw to that list, incidentally. I think I've probably done enough scolding, indirectly, in my writings.

Zebrowski: What, if anything, would you like me to ask you that I did not ask?

Clarke: Frankly, I can't think of one, but perhaps by the time

---

7   Clarke shared his home in Sri Lanka with Hector Ekanayake, his wife Valerie, and the couple's three daughters. Hector Ekanayake's brother Leslie, one of Clarke's closest friends, a fellow diver, and a partner in his business ventures, died in a motorcycle accident in 1977.

we get closer to publication I may have thought of one. I see that I finished taping these answers on the morning of the 29th of December 1998, while waiting for Valerie and the two younger girls to come back from Egypt, bringing back lots of photographs and full of stories.

Zebrowski: One final question, and I think you can guess what it's about. In this year of 2001, what are your thoughts about the movie? Seems it's a long, long science fictional way from E. E. Smith's Arisian patron race, via your Overlords in *Childhood's End*, to the subtle cosmic engineers of *2001: A Space Odyssey*.

Clarke: Having just seen the Special Edition Stanley has been working on for the last five years of his life: it couldn't have been done better even now—merely in a tenth of the time, thanks to today's computers!

Arthur Clarke, over and out.

An Interview with
JAMES GUNN

George Zebrowski: What did you think you were doing when you started writing?

James Gunn: I started several times, at different points in my life and for different reasons. The first time was when I was in kindergarten and wrote a two line verse. It was doggerel, but my father, a printer, thought it was remarkable and printed it on a card. That may have been my first realization that the purpose of writing is to get published. I suspect that it was motivated by my discovery of reading maybe a year earlier. It was "Farmer Brown's Boy Sees a Bear," and the magic of seeing marks on a page become words infected me with a love for language that stayed with me the rest of my life.

The next point, after years of reading almost everything from works of art to pulp magazines (and it was the pulp magazines that had the greatest impact, beginning when I was ten and my father brought home the first Doc Savage magazine that may have convinced me that writing narratives like this was ordinary activity that anybody could do), my parents bought me a used portable typewriter, a Smith-Corona with a lever on the right side that raised the keys into typing position. That unleashed the pleasure of seeing my writing transformed into book or magazine-like words on a page and made it more real. I used it for writing school assignments (and during World War II carried it with me everywhere I was sent, mostly to write letters but sometimes verse and articles) and, when I was 16, a science fiction story that I sent to *Astounding*, got rejected, and has mercifully been lost (I don't remember what it was about). My motive then was simply to get published.

I wrote radio plays in high school (there was an organization called "the Safety Pins") and papers, and contributed to a student magazine when I was a sophomore in junior college, but my first real experience with publication came when I was a junior in journalism at the University of Kansas, where I wrote news stories for the student newspaper but, more importantly, columns and editorials and feature articles and occasional verse and saw them published. I chose journalism because I had already decided that writing would be my profession, and the only model I had for people getting paid to be writers was newspaper reporters.

Then, after the War, in my senior year, I wrote a lot of editorials for the University *Daily Kansan* as well as feature articles, but I also wrote a stage play for a playwriting class that got produced by the University Theater (and gave me the illusion that I had a future as a playwright), but I also wrote a feature article about the colorful professor who taught the class (and directed and acted in the University Theater) that got published in the *Kansas City Star*. I also wrote a sonnet in a poetry-writing class that I got published in the "Moonbeams" column of the *Kansas City Star*. The article and the poem were the first things I actually got paid for ($15 for the article, $10 for the poem), and that was a revelation, too. Part of my motivation got transformed from simply seeing my writing in print to getting paid for it.

That playwriting success led me to Northwestern University for graduate study, but after a couple of quarters I realized that I wasn't getting anywhere with playwriting and didn't want an advanced degree in theater, but I did find radio writing exciting. So I went back to Kansas City with the idea of writing a series of radio plays based on Kansas City history—and found that no K.C. radio station was interested. That was in 1948 and television had not yet reached Kansas City but was clearly in sight. So, sitting in a third-story living space (actually a garret), I decided to write something I might be able to sell—a science fiction story. I had fallen in love with science fiction at the age of six or seven when I discovered a treasure-trove of Tarzan novels in my grandmother's back closet where my literature-loving uncles (or maybe my more adventure-story-loving father) had consigned them. I had already read my way through the fairytale books in my grade-school library as well as the Dr. Doolittle books and a bunch of historical novels, but Edgar Rice Burroughs was different. And then, when I was eleven, I discovered a used-magazine store in downtown Kansas City and in its dusty back shelves stacks of magazines with names like *Amazing Stories, Wonder Stories*, and *Astounding Stories of Super Science*. I not only could trade two of my hero pulp magazines for one of those, but I found in them stories just as adventurous but with a quality of ideation that elevated them into the rarified space of originality that appealed to me. I also fell in love with fantasy when I was 16 and *Famous Fantastic Mysteries* appeared on the newsstands with all of the old Munsey pulp reprints of A. Merritt and other early 20th century authors. But that was pleasure reading and science fiction was real. And what was also real was that I had a wife to support and dwindling savings from my wartime service.

So I sat down at my typewriter (now an L. C. Smith standard) and wrote a science fiction story, "Paradox," sent it to John Campbell at *Astounding*, got a one-line typed rejection, sent it to *Amazing Stories* and got a standard rejection, and sent it to *Thrilling Wonder Stories* and one day got a letter from the editor, Sam Merwin, Jr., saying, "I like your story 'Paradox' and I'll pay you $80 for it." That was a revelation and a turning point. Someone would actually pay me to sit in front of a typewriter and turn the inside of my head into stories. I liked both parts of that, writing the stories and being paid to do it.

But not enough. I sold only three stories that year and decided to go back to the University to get an advanced degree, which might allow me to get a teaching job to support my writing habit and would provide a stipend under the G.I. Bill to pay the bills in the meantime. As it turned out, I sold nine of the first ten stories I wrote, when the burgeoning magazine market of the early 1950s took the other six. My first two stories were published in the fall of 1949, and I was the only published author in the small graduate-student class in the English Department. In the second year I wrote a science fiction play as an "Investigation and Conference" project in order to turn it into a novella that I could send off to a new science fiction magazine, *Galaxy*. It was "Breaking Point" and it earned me a telephone call from Horace Gold who said he liked it but it was too long and asked me if he could have Ted Sturgeon cut it by a third. I said okay, stunned a bit by my first personal contact with an editor; it didn't work out and got published in Lester del Rey's *Space Science Fiction*, but the entire experience left me feeling that somehow I had put a foot into the doorway of recognition and accomplishment. I might even write a novel.

But all of this is merely preface to what the question really addressed—my first real career decision about writing and what I thought I was doing. Everything before that was preface. After getting my master's degree in 1951, I accepted an editing position with Western Printing & Lithographing Company of Racine, Wisconsin, which edited and published the Dell line of paperbacks, and in the late summer of 1952 I persuaded the editor-in-chief to send me to the World Science Fiction Convention meeting that year in Chicago. That experience was a life-changer. I met some of my writing heroes, Jack Williamson (standing behind me in the registration line), Clifford Simak, and others, met some new ones like Bob Bloch and Mack Reynolds, and saw John Campbell and Tony Boucher from a few feet away and Hugo Gernsback, Willy Ley, and Ray Palmer. Perhaps more important, I met Fred Pohl, who had become my agent, and he told me he had sold four stories for me, and on the feeble strength of that information I went back to Racine, quit my job, and decided to resume my writing career.

Because it was going to be a career, one that hasn't stopped since. It was going to be a life, a way of life, a reason for life. Part of the conversion was the feeling that I got from the convention that I had become part of something. I was accepted into a brotherhood, part of what H. G. Wells called an "Open Conspiracy" when he spoke in Kansas City in 1937, a talk my uncle John took me and my brother Richard to hear, and we pressed forward through crowds taller and bigger than us but the great man brushed past us without noticing. There was within that hall in the Morrison Hotel a dedication to something larger than the number of people (fewer than a thousand) gathered in it, and I left wanting to deserve my place in that distinguished and dedicated company. I have felt that way ever since, and it led, eventually, to the motto with which I began to sign my letters and messages in the last couple of decades, "Let's save the world through science fiction."

Zebrowski: From among your early stories, published/and or unpublished, which do you like best, or have special thoughts about?

Gunn: The first story I sold to John Campbell's *Astounding*, "Private Enterprise," stands out because it was my third story and getting published in *Astounding* fulfilled a long-held goal. It wasn't that great a story, but seeing it in the July 1950 issue was a good feeling.

The first story I sold to *Galaxy* was another accomplishment I felt good about. *Galaxy* had come along, with its sophisticated social science fiction and replaced, in part anyway, *Astounding* in my heart, and "The Misogynist," the first story I sold under my own name and the eleventh I wrote, had what was, for me, an innovate framework. Horace Gold liked it enough to insert his own ending, but I restored my own in the *Future Imperfect* reprint.

"Wherever You May Be," in the May 1953 *Galaxy*, was my first lead novella, and I had a lot of fun writing it. One of the few stories that seemed to write itself. I retitled it "The Reluctant Witch" when it was reprinted in *The Witching Hour.* And it almost got made into a movie three times (and did get filmed, with no permission, in the Soviet Union).

I liked "Name Your Pleasure," which was published in the Winter 1955 *Thrilling Wonder Stories,* because it turned a philosophical musing about happiness into a successful novella that became the central portion (that I renamed "The Hedonist") of my novel *The Joy Makers.*

I liked "Little Orphan Android," which was published in the September 1955 *Galaxy*, because it was a change of pace as a comic response to Fred Pohl's "The Midas Plague"—and I really liked the title.

"New Blood" in the October 1955 *Astounding* was important to me because it launched the series of stories that became *The Immortals*, which not only sold nearly 200,000 copies for Bantam Books but got dramatized as an ABC-TV movie of the week and a TV series the following year, and much later got a series of options to turn it (unsuccessfully) into a feature film. It did get adapted as a feature film (without permission) by the Great Wall Film Company of Hong Kong.

But perhaps the single story I felt best about was "The Cave of Night" in the February 1955 *Galaxy.* I considered it my *"Saturday Evening Post"* story, and Fred Pohl, my agent at the time, sent it around to the *Post*, but when it got rejected shipped it over to *Galaxy.* It had some success there, as one of my four X Minus One radio dramatizations and then a Desilu Playhouse presentation as "Man in Orbit," but mostly I liked it because it was slickly written, which was kind of ironic because Horace wanted *Galaxy* to be the *Saturday Evening Post* of the science fiction world.

Zebrowski: Do you write in the direction of what you like to read, or are the two different? How different?

Gunn: I have been shaped by the reading I have done since my earliest days, but I think it has influenced my writing only in technical ways, that is, in ways of handling scenes and transitions. With a couple of exceptions, I have never tried to consciously emulate any other writer's style or concepts. Of course one cannot evaluate unconscious influences, but mostly my story ideas have been sufficiently off the beaten path and their grasp on my imagination and need to write them have been sufficient to shape my writing of them.

Zebrowski: In all fiction, who are the authors you admire?

Gunn: I started in the second grade with Andrew Lang's fairytale books and Hugh Lofting's Dr. Doolittle books, graduated to Edgar Rice Burroughs's Tarzan novels, the early magazine science fiction writers in the days when I wasn't paying much attention to who they were, and then, from the library, H. G. Wells, Conan Doyle. H. Rider Haggard, and Jules Verne. I moved outside the genre authors to read the historical novelists, particularly Kenneth Roberts and Thomas Costain, and then among my teenage passions, Thomas Wolfe.

In science fiction, I admired Jack Williamson and Clifford Simak, then Robert Heinlein and Theodore Sturgeon, A. E. van Vogt and Isaac Asimov, and finally Fred Pohl , Cyril Kornbluth, Alfred Bester, and Henry Kuttner and C. L Moore, particularly their collaborations. I'm sure I've forgotten some, particularly the humorists like Robert Sheckley, Fredric Brown, and Phil Klass, as well as others, such as Ursula K. Le Guin, whose individual works I may admire more than everything they wrote.

Zebrowski: Lester del Rey was once asked where he stood as a writer. "In the forefront of the second rank!" he answered. Isn't this where we all stand, in all likelihood?

Gunn: I'd agree with Lester (and you). Being in the first rank is something that is conferred rather than claimed, and my feeling is that I have worked away on various projects that have seized my attention and completed them in ways that were personally satisfying and sometimes things that no one else was doing or hadn't done yet and in ways that represented what I told my fiction writing students was the only thing worth writing: what only you can write. Certainly I don't feel I belong in the ranks of the authors I listed above as those I admired.

It's difficult to imagine what my writing career would have been like if I had continued my free-lance writing that lasted from late 1952 to 1955, but I got drawn into other university services that culminated in twenty-three years of teaching and writing plus a good deal of both in retirement. One consequence was that my writing time was more limited but also I only worked on projects that I really wanted to write rather than being tempted to write stuff because I needed the income.

I've been lucky in some ways—the television adaptations of "The Cave of Night" and *The Immortals* are two of them—and in finding editors who liked my writing and found ways to publish it: Dick Roberts at Bantam Books, David Hartwell at several different publishers, Norbert Slepyan at Scribner's, Fred Pohl as magazine and book editor, Stan Schmidt and Sheila Williams at their respective magazines. But I never quite achieved that breakout or best-selling book, in spite of the fact that a number of my later books were more social commentary than science fiction. Of particular disappointment was the novel I worked on for twenty years, *The Millennium Blues*, which I thought of as my purely "literary" novel for the general audience and got published only as a collector's edition and print-on-demand.

So the second rank seems like an appropriate place, and I have good company.

Zebrowski: Science fiction has been described as a "premature" literary form, a "sooner," if anyone nowadays knows what that old term out of American history means. I have described SF as a rehearsal of possible futures. Einstein held that past, present, and future are fixed, illusory to our psychology. Maybe an infinity of futures are what is fixed, which makes the idea more palatable. Stanislaw Lem once said that science fiction interested him more as a phenomenon rather than for its literary claims. John W. Campbell made the literary claim, that science fiction was the mainline of literature and that contemporary fictions were the specialized form of science fiction. Barry Malzberg once remarked that few of us among writers and readers understand science fiction's importance. And you have voiced the motto "Save the World Through Science Fiction," suggesting that the attitudes in science fictional speculation may help our human project.

Nowadays we see this imaginative attitude spreading out among non-genre writers, the media, and serious comic book writers. Science fiction's terminology has spread into common language, well beyond readers. Fantasy has become a giant larger than what might be defined as "real" science fiction, which in Arthur C. Clarke's words is "about things that may actually happen." But he also said that "to see what might be possible one must go a ways beyond the possible." A few scientists have complained that there is too much science fiction in science and not enough science in the science fiction.

Given all these claims and considerations, what do you think is going on?

Gunn: Big questions for which any answers must be tentative. I'm not as certain about anything as the authorities you quote. Granted that, let me quote Isaac Asimov from nearly 45 years ago: "We live in a science fiction world." He meant that the world of the early 1970s, with its spaceships, moon landing, atomic bombs and atomic energy, the beginnings of robot industrial production, and the growing importance of science and technology was very much like the world that he and others were writing about in 1939 and the 1940s. But that description applies even more to our contemporary world, with its social media, explorations of other planets, and the everyday reality of our world, where each new development or discovery is compared to science fiction and has the potential to influence human lives. (And in other ways, such as the political and social, the world we are living in may be more like fantasy or even horror.)

The world of science fiction writing and publishing has undergone its own transformation, with increasing commercialization and monetizing and coarsening of the marketplace typified by the comicons and the proliferation of the comic-book film exploitations. Traditional publishing and traditional book selling are being threatened by digital publishing and internet distribution. The magazines, which once were a central part of science fiction identity and a major factor in genre change, are now a shadow of their former influence and circulation. I have a theory that science fiction has been re-imagined every dozen years by the arrival of a major editor (or in 1949 and 1950 more than one), but the last such change occurred in 1964 and later transformations have worked with less direction and more chaos. In the midst of plenty, with book publication in the U.S. around 3,000 titles a year and "sci-fi" films and TV series continuing to proliferate and even dominate, science fiction is drowning in surfeit.

With all this confusion and lack of focus in the field, some great work continues to be published, but it's difficult to find in the welter. And the proliferation, which provides an income (even a living income for a few best-sellers) for more authors, also means the proliferation of different fandoms so that there no longer is common ground or common understanding, and political disputes arise. I no longer am able to keep up with contemporary fiction, both for lack of time and macular degeneration, but I still read the finalists for the Sturgeon award. What I notice is greater skill in writing and smaller concepts or none at all. Many are excellent explorations of human relationships but are science fiction only to provide a pivot for those relationships and fail Ted Sturgeon's definition of science fiction as a story that wouldn't have happened without the scientific content. They could as easily be written using any other MacGuffin.

In the midst of all this, with film and TV tie-in novels competing and outselling all but a few of the most popular titles (and even an association of media tie-in writers), the mid-list book has mostly been turned over to the small presses. And the mid-list books were where most of the innovative works once were published.

With all these issues complicating today's science fiction, why do I continue to suggest "Let's save the world through science fiction"? In spite of everything, I feel that science fiction still has something to offer that other kinds of fiction do not; even in all but the most degraded form science fiction still asks its readers to consider the premises of its speculation, the implicit or explicit analysis and commentary on current conditions, and the possibility of change. Its readers have to think rather than simply surrender themselves to the narrative.

But that is only part of it. I also speculate that reading science fiction calls upon the prefrontal lobes, the rational part of the brain, and I have been trying to work with psychologists to measure that effect with neuroscience imaging. If we could prove that science fiction actually exercises a different part of the brain from, say, the adventure story, the romance, the fantasy, the horror story, and even the mainstream story, and that it might even change the brain, the way London cabbies reportedly have had their brains changed by their memorization of London streets, we might be able to encourage the reading of science fiction for its influences as well as its pleasures, to introduce the reading of science fiction at early ages, in and out of classrooms, and rear a more rational, thoughtful generation that could produce a more rational, thoughtful society. Failing to get funding for a real experiment, I even wrote a story about it for *Analog*, "Saving the World."

I recognize that rather than changing brains and thinking patterns, such MRI tests might show, instead, that science fiction readers are people who already have brains structured to read and respond to science fiction, but even that would be useful information. Letting science fiction readers change the world would be a remarkable, Asimovian experiment.

Zebrowski: There is that which has been described as the "writerly" way of creating fiction, beyond the crude recitation of a story line. James Blish once told me that it was required that a "hard" SF story be hard in its thinking and in its prose. You once told me that SF publishers do not permit SF to be as "writerly" in its prose as it permits contemporary fiction. And within the genre a praise for prose has often been looked down upon, despite the presence of a Theodore Sturgeon, an Edgar Pangborn, or a James Blish, even as far back as H. G. Wells. Pangborn's prose has been dismissed as excessive, while Orwell has been charged with lacking in distinction.

Has any of this changed? Isn't SF by its nature innovative, and demanding less of it strange while complaining when it gives more? How should this problem be stated, if at all?

Gunn: That's the issue, isn't it? Ideas or craft, concepts or style? You call it "writerly." That covers a broad spectrum of creative work, from the handling of situation and character to a concern for language and sentence, as well as a focus on thematic concerns for today's understanding of the human condition as opposed to science fiction's concern for whatever the human condition may become. I think that is what differentiates classic science fiction from today's science fiction—which is prioritized, story or treatment? Ideally, some of us would prefer both, and some of us, you and me and others such as Sturgeon and Pangborn and Blish tried to accomplish both. But as far back as the early days of *Amazing Stories*, when Gernsback was filling the magazine with reprints from Poe, Verne, and Wells, readers were beginning to chafe at "literary dawdling," as one reader complained, in the October 1927 issue, about Wells "using too many words to describe a situation."

The dichotomy between story and style has played itself out through the history of the genre, but it got new energy from the emergence of the new wave in the pages of Michael Moorcock's *New Worlds*, when writers like J. G. Ballard, Brian Aldiss, and others plotted a rebellion against Campbellesque SF. It was a culmination of the gradual demolition of the ghetto walls between science fiction and the mainstream, with an infiltration of science fiction tropes into the mainstream and a seeping of mainstream values into science fiction. Maybe this trend has been accelerated by the development of workshops like Clarion, Milford, and here at the University of Kansas, as well as the availability of fiction-writing programs in general, the proliferation of MFAs, and the gradual acceptance of genre writing in academia.

I remember a conversation with Christopher Priest in my hotel room in London, where I was staying for a few days after the founding meeting of World SF in Ireland, when Priest spoke about putting away childish things in his writing and I championed remaining in touch with my youthful loves. Certainly it has worked for Priest in his later career, and I have ventured outside genre boundaries a few times myself in novels such as *Kampus* and *The Millennium Blues*. But my ambition, as I wrote in the introduction to one of my collections of stories, was to write science fiction with literary skills. And I wasn't alone in that.

These days, with the lowering of the distinctions between science fiction and fantasy (which Damon Knight never thought existed) in categories like the New Weird and a growing body of well-written, character-driven stories and novels in which the science fiction element is present only peripherally, like one of Hitchcock's McGuffins, one can sense boundaries crumbling into mere mounds. This is not to pick sides—despite personal preference for "idea" science fiction written well—because I've always believed that science fiction belonged to whoever wanted to use it, the ghetto-dwellers and the teachers in the classroom, the filmmakers, the TV writers, the comic-book artists, the game players, the fan and the casual reader. I've championed an understanding of the historical development of science fiction over the ages as a background for reading and writing today's fiction, but I recognize that it can as easily and legitimately be used to look at science fiction as a source of ideas, as great books, for teaching science, history, anthropology, or sociology.

But what I see in today's fiction is excellently-written stories that lack the excitement of idea I found in its earlier days. I noticed recently the cluster of transformative novels in the early 1950s, particularly between 1952 and 1954. When I inspected the twenty-five novels I assigned in my science fiction novel class, I found that more than half-a-dozen of them were published during that period.

We'll have to wait for another decade or so to see what science fiction becomes. In its first forty years it changed every dozen years, as a new editor emerged with a new vision and gathered writers around him who responded to his vision. The magazines have diminished as gatekeepers and genre-changers, and the burgeoning book market has difficulty instigating any general revolution. Traditional publishing may die; digital publication or social media may become the major influences, or whatever replaces them. It would be interesting to hang around to see.

Zebrowski: One of the more honest editors once said to me, "Whether we publish your book or not has nothing to do with its merits." Another said that merit can only be glimpsed out of the corner of your eye, so the best measure we have of it is sales. And Stephen Colbert has mocked, "If it made money, it's a good book." Merit is not to be risked by editors afraid for their jobs. This tyranny has never been complete. Some authors would bring great shame down on the house if they were run off the reservation. What all this confesses cannot be avoided: editors are horse players, and their guesses are to be suspected. But it's gotten worse; recently, a generation of SF writers cannot get a novel accepted. "Well, what do you expect," runs the question, "that we pick losers?"

Might as well pick merit rather than blame the horses, since all the means of sale are in the hands of publishers, who do everything for the few and nearly nothing for the many. One example occurred when a writer's contract stated a set amount would be set aside for publicity; when he finally noticed that the money hadn't been spent on promotion, he was told that it was now too late to do so.

Why does this state of affairs still exist? Money—although it has been hotly denied, then admitted when the editor loses his job. SF's best editors were mostly writers, who were driven out when they "lost" money. Would money have made any difference? No, most books lose money for lack of an audience and/or promotion.

We should affirm a principle. All works of merit should be published, and there is enough evidence to show that they are likely to do as well as the race-fixing choices of the money men, or if they were chosen by lottery from among the gifted.

Do you think that perhaps something like this is coming about—by a science fictional means, e-publishing and print on demand—leaving time to sort out the merits? Yet here too, the monetizers are moving in with their notion of "catered" fiction.

Don't you think that risking merit, with no other motive, is actually not much of a risk?

Gunn: I had a very good editor—Frederik Pohl—tell me once about a novel I had submitted to him (actually a chapter and a proposal), "I think I know how to publish this." It may not be the only criterion but an important one: an editor imagines himself publishing a book in a certain way and that leads to an acceptance. The book was *Kampus*, and it was not a traditional science fiction novel. Although it used one of Heinlein's three plots—the Man who learned better—the protagonist was a student in a future, student-run university, and the theme of the novel was how the culture might have turned out if the student rebels of the Sixties had been successful, using Voltaire's *Candide* as a structural model. I don't think any science fiction editor but Fred would have accepted it. It sold moderately well, but not as well as Chip Delany's *Dhalgren*. Fred mentioned both books in his autobiographical essay in *Contemporary Authors Autobiography Series*, volume one.

Years later, when I wrote another hard-to-categorize novel, *The Millennium Blues*, about the coming end of the second millennium, I was aiming at the mainstream audience with what I thought would be my literary and maybe my bestseller work. I worked on it, off and on, for twenty years. I never found a Fred Pohl in the mainstream or in the science fiction field either who "knew" how they could publish it (one editor was going to publish it but his firm went out of business). So it got published as print-on-demand and, ironically, in a collector's edition.

It may be that there aren't enough insightful editors, or maybe enough with good imaginations, or simply, as I think is true, every book with merit—which usually means a well-written novel about something new and exciting—needs to find an editor who knows how to publish it, and sometimes it must go through a lot of editorial hands before it finds one. If it ever does.

That, at least, is the way it used to be. A few decades back the system that had prevailed for generations—I envision it as the Maxwell Perkins era, the age of Faulkner, Hemingway, and most of all Thomas Wolfe—was one in which an editor accepted a book on merit and the salesmen took it out to bookstores who ordered copies. Then the big book store chains came along, and the sales people began catering to their orders, because they were selling half of all the books published, and if they didn't order copies the book would be a financial risk if not a loss. And the chain stores began to keep records of sales and would order fewer copies of authors whose work sold less well, until the sales forces began consulting with chain store buyers before the book was even accepted, and then the sales people, who hadn't read the book (or maybe any book) had to be consulted about any new book that was submitted before an editor could get a contract approved, and the auditors had to cost a book out as a moneymaker.

Everyone has horror stories: I remember a contract I had with Harper & Row, back in the days when novels came in and out of print, to edit a series of classic science fiction texts for classrooms, complete with introductions and academic apparatus—and I had a couple of classics lined up, which had its difficulties when the classics were still in print elsewhere (but this is where I wanted to start). One of these was A. E. van Vogt's *The World of Null-A*, and I had persuaded Damon Knight, who had written a scathing review back in 1945, to write the introduction with what, I hoped, would be a new appraisal. But then I got a letter from the editor telling me that the sales people had determined that they couldn't sell a book that would cost twenty-five cents more than another edition. The contract for the series got cancelled.

On another occasion I sat in the office of David Hartwell at Pocket Books who told me that the sales people had determined that it would cost Pocket Books as much to reprint *The Joy Makers* as to cancel it, so it got canceled. The situation, if anything, seems to be even worse these days. Before my recent novel *Transcendental* got a contract, the editor had to get the approval of the sales force and the bookkeepers. And I had responses from other editors saying, "We can't publish this kind of intelligent novel any more" and "I could have published this ten years ago but not today."

In an ideal world an editor should be a person with literary appreciation, a background in the field, and publishing understanding, and should make a decision about whether a book meets the standards of the publisher and the field and is worth publishing. And then the publisher should publish it in the most effective and attractive way and the sales people should go out and sell it.

If there's any satisfaction in irony, today the chain book stores are either bankrupt or in trouble, websites are selling more books than bookstores, digital publishing and self-publishing are threatening traditional methods, and publishers aren't sure what their world will be like in a decade or two.

Zebrowski: In your list of "transformative" novels that you recently sent to me are a few that did not find publishers easily or for large sums. They all shine through in one way of another. Another list or two like this one of lasting works might be made.

Here's the list you sent. Would you answer with a few words about each of these books?

Gunn: It's true. I chose these books because they were the ones I selected for my course in the science fiction novel. The novel course, like the short-story course, was intended to focus on how the genre became what it is. There are other approaches possible, particularly what I call the "great books" course; but great books, by their very nature, are unique—at least until they influence later works. The books I selected had elements of greatness but also contributions to the development of the genre. And I noticed then that they curiously clustered around the period of the early 1950s. I had novels by H. G. Wells, a couple from the 1940s, and a number from the 1960s and later, but the 1950s were exceptional. Maybe it was the entry of *Galaxy Science Fiction* into the field, with Horace Gold's encouragement of social science fiction, but *Astounding* was invigorated too, and *The Magazine of Fantasy & Science Fiction* had a contribution to make as well. Ballantine Books entered the picture then, and the book market was picking up elsewhere, with Doubleday, Simon and Schuster, and others, including the fan presses. Maybe it helped that this was my period of freelancing after discovering the inner world of science fiction by attending my first science fiction convention, which happened to be the 1952 World Science Fiction Convention in Chicago.

Transformative novels published between 1952 and 1955:

The Caves of Steel. A lot of readers and critics consider other Isaac Asimov novels as his best and the Foundation trilogy was generically important, but I always liked *The Caves of Steel* as a significant contribution to the burgeoning social science fiction field combined with intellectual rigor. Many of Asimov's stories and novels take place on bare stages, but here the vast metropolis under its massive dome is fully realized, his characters have real lives and even R. Daneel Olivaw seems as real as the people (maybe more real), and the Darwinian issues raised by the novel—the growth of the metropolis and its effect on the lives and character of its citizens, the problem of robots and human workers, the effect of the Spacers' extended lives and their dependence on robots, and the need for human expansion into the galaxy are all wound up in an appropriate murder mystery.

Mission of Gravity. Hal Clement's masterpiece showed that a focus on hard science could be combined with characterization of aliens who are believable products of their environment. One can trace Clement's influence down through Larry Niven, Gregory Benford, Greg Bear, David Brin, and others.

The Demolished Man. Galaxy established its tone with two 1952 serials. This was one of them. Alfred Bester was writing marvelous short stories, most of which were appearing in the *Magazine of Fantasy & Science Fiction*, but this novel about murder in a world of telepathic detectives was marvelously imagined and richly detailed. It was the first of its kind and showed that it could be done.

The Space Merchants. The second 1952 *Galaxy* serial was Frederik Pohl and Cyril Kornbluth's first collaboration since their Futurian days, and it broke new ground by naturalizing satire. Up until this time satire was clearly an intellectual exercise in a world detached from reality. *The Space Merchants* created a believable science fiction world while still pointing out the dangers and follies of advertising, and would lead to further fruitful collaborations until Kornbluth's untimely death.

Childhood's End. Arthur Clarke expanded his short story "Guardian Angel" into a novel that coped with the satanic image with which the story ended (although it is said that James Blish contributed the ending), with all its Paradise Lost implications. It was the other, visionary side of Clarke's work, and it demonstrated that spiritual concerns could be considered in a thoroughly science-fictional way.

The Puppet Masters. All of Robert Heinlein's 1950s novels are meaningful, and his contributions to craft and message permeate the field to this day, but in this novel, it always seemed to me, he managed to incorporate his political message about the nature of human responsibility into an artistic narrative more seamlessly than in any other.

More Than Human. Theodore Sturgeon was a natural short-story writer, and it may be significant that his best novel, and one that showed how psychological concepts could be integrated into an effective science-fictional treatment of his typical social outcasts, was a combination of three linked novellas. His "Baby Is Three," the middle section, was a shocking success in *Galaxy*, and is a further reminder of how the early years of the magazine provided one remarkable accomplishment after another.

And others that weren't on my reading list:

The Long Loud Silence—Bob Tucker's naturalistic treatment of atomic catastrophe.

Earth Abides—George R. Stewart's quietly literary treatment of the struggle to survive after a devastating virus illustrates that not all meaningful work was coming out of the science fiction field. Actually it was published in 1949, just short of the Fifties.

City—Clifford Simak's novel-like collection of his short stories about human abandonment of Earth, leaving it to the dogs.

Brain Wave—Poul Anderson's first novel, about Earth emerging from a portion of space that inhibits mental ability.

The Martian Chronicles—The collection of Ray Bradbury's mixed bag of stories about human expeditions to Mars that established his reputation, created a market for personal and poetic visions, and has rarely been out of print since.

Bring the Jubilee—With this novel, serialized as I recall in *The Magazine of Fantasy & Science Fiction*, Ward Moore brought the alternate history back from its earlier treatments gathered in J. C. Squires's *If It Had Happened Otherwise*, and made it a part of the science fiction field that has become a genre in its own right.

Starman's Son—Andre Norton's first novel that launched a long career.

And a fantasy, *Conjure Wife*. Fritz Leiber may be better known for his heroic fantasy, but this novel of everyday magic on a college campus is a masterpiece and may have been a major inspiration for the rise of urban fantasy.

Zebrowski: I notice that you swore off being a full time writer in the 1950s, although your short fiction continued being published in the magazines, with one story reaching major television adaptation. But when you became more prolific in the 1970s with both paperback and hardcover publication, this period coincided with a sudden upsurge of serious SF being published by the major houses, by writers who came in during the 1970s. I attribute this to the editors who felt close to the ambitions of these writers, until it became clear that few of them made any impressive amounts of money. And so the gap between ambitious editors and their writers widened. But for a while you and other authors had it their way, with handsome prominent editions, until the desert came back, making merit impotent before the ulterior motives of profit. The free play of imagination was slowed, leaving talent compromised or silent.

Self-directed writers are slowed or silenced by the marketplace run by agents and editors loyal to the publishers. Corporations own the stomachs of writers, many of whom are content to become technicians, able craftsmen providing what is wanted. The expectations fostered by the submission invitations of publishers have become a feared contract, leading houses to demand one-way agented submissions only, ignoring the cultural contract, which one day clever lawyers will rediscover. What this has meant is that dozens of gifted SF writers, who have developed strongly, are mostly locked out by editors fearful of difficulties with genuine talents. Small presses, e-books, and print on demand editions have taken up some slack, but they are forced to compete with the bean counters; some stop publishing, others rush to the bottom with the major pirates.

Is it not fair to say that full time authors live in a censorious enslavement, where merit has little to do with whether an author is published or not?

Gunn: I didn't "swear off" full-time writing in 1955. Aftet two and a half years as a full-time writer (after an earlier trial run as a freelance writer in 1948-49), my family moved back to Lawrence, Kansas, where my wife and I had both earned bachelor's degrees and I had earned an M.A., because Jane, who had grown up in a small north-central Kansas town, didn't like living in Kansas City. But I fully intended continuing my developing career as a full-time writer. Then events intervened.

I went in to talk to James Wortham, the chair of the English department, and he told me that he had two sections of freshman English for which he didn't have an instructor and asked if I would be willing to teach them. I said I would, but I continued to write. Before the semester was over, Wortham called me into his office and said that Fred Ellsworth, the executive secretary of the Alumni Association, was looking for an editor for the alumni magazine, and I went over to talk to him. He offered me the job and I accepted on the condition that I could take a week off every month and a month off in the summer to do my own writing. I might add that my income from both jobs was more than I was making as a full-time writer.

It was during this period of editing the alumni publications that I completed (and published separately the individual sections) of *Station in Space*, *The Joy Makers*, and *The Immortals*, and put together the stories for the *Future Imperfect* collection. By that time, in 1958, I was called into Ellsworth's office to learn that the Chancellor's office wanted to know if I'd take a job writing feature articles about the University, and I agreed to do that. I did write a few things in that position, including a screenplay adaptation of "The Reluctant Witch," but my production was dwindling. By the end of that year, I was called into the Chancellor's office, to be told that he was going to give me a raise of $1,000 (which was almost a 20% raise). By the time I got back to the converted storeroom that was my office, I got another call from the Chancellor who told me he was going to create the new position of Administrative Assistant to the Chancellor for University Relations and would I be interested. I said I would and he said he'd add another $500 to my pay.

It was during this period of creating a new position and learning how to do it during a period of student and national unrest, culminating in protests and demonstrations on racial and then Vietnam War issues, that I had no time for writing. The only thing I wrote (except for the articles and speeches I was writing for the University) was "The Old Folks," which I tricked myself into writing by offering sections as examples for the class in fiction writing I was teaching. I had difficulty selling it until I encountered Harry Harrison at the World Science Fiction Convention in Berkeley in 1968 (where I made my return to science fiction), he asked me for a story for his new original anthology *Nova*, and I said I had this story that the slick magazines rejected because they didn't publish science fiction and the science fiction magazines rejected because it wasn't science fiction. He said categories didn't bother him and published it and reprinted it in his and Brian Aldiss's best-of-the-year volume.

By then I had decided that I needed to get back to writing science fiction again, and in August of 1967 I took, for the first time, the month vacation to which I was entitled, and worked on manuscripts that I had been planning in the previous months, finishing the two novellas that completed *The Burning* (and sold them to Fred Pohl for *If* and *Galaxy*), and in the following two Augusts wrote other stories and, most important, the first chapter of *The Listeners* (called "The Listeners," which I also sold to Fred at *Galaxy*) and the second chapter of *Kampus*. These, I feel were the product of a growing maturity in vision and writing skills and maybe a result of storing up writing energy over the previous seven or eight years of abstinence.

If I was aware of a similar maturity in the field as a whole, I don't remember it, but perhaps it drifted down into my consciousness. By 1970 I had decided I had done everything I could with University Relations and wanted to get back to my own writing, so I asked the English Department if it wanted me as a full-time colleague. The chair of the department came to my office and said that the department had voted unanimously that it would welcome me and that "some of the younger members of the department hope you will be willing to teach a course in science fiction."

Going back to teaching released a great deal of creative energy. I published one or two books a year for the next few years and every year or so thereafter, novels, collections, anthologies, and nonfiction works about science fiction, as well as articles, introductions, and other short scholarly work. I also got involved with organizational work, first as president of SFWA and then of SFRA (Science Fiction Research Association).

The first solid sign that science fiction had entered into a new stage of mainstream acceptance was when I learned that Scribner's was creating a new science fiction line, and my agent Bob Hoskins of Scott Meredith's agency, where I wound up for a couple of years after I left Harry Altshuler over "The Listeners" and Bob Mills (who would wind up as my agent later but didn't like that story either) sent "The Listeners" to Norman Slepyan. That was my introduction to mainstream publishing. It didn't pay any better than genre publishing—a $2,000 advance; I got $2,500 from Bantam Books a decade earlier—but the ambience was out of a young writer's literary dreams. After that came the interest of Harper & Row and then Pocket Books under David Hartwell. In between, there was the interest of such mainline publishers as Prentice-Hall, Mentor Books, and Oxford University Press in my academic publications.

It seems to me now that the field was transformed in the late 1960s and early 1970s when my novel *The Listeners* was published. Two agents had, as I mentioned, responded negatively to the novelette (also called "The Listeners") and I only got that story published in *Galaxy* because Fred Pohl saw something in it that they didn't. In fact, it may have been unpublishable in an earlier period. Fred was a good editor; I don't think anybody else would have published *Kampus*, as Fred did a few years later at Bantam. And Norbert Slepyan was the editor who accepted *The Listeners* at Scribner's.

Looking back I'd say that maybe it began with Le Guin's *The Left Hand of Darkness*. Silverberg's *Dying Inside* was another outlier, although it was probably intended as a mainstream novel. Maybe these novels and others were "literary" enough to have been published anyway. But it was more than being literary. There had developed within the science fiction community, authors and readers and editors, an acceptance of different ways to shape narratives and different aspects of life to reflect.

I know that when I returned to writing in the late 1960s, when I finally took the month's vacation to which I was entitled during my public relations days and devoted Augusts to writing, my writing had changed, matured, and the ideas that came to me arrived in different forms.

Up to this point the significant changes in science fiction had occurred in the magazines. Looking back, this may have been the point at which the field began to be shaped by the novels.

It wasn't until Frank Herbert, Robert Heinlein, and Jerry Pournelle and Larry Niven broke the genre ceiling into best-seller categories that writing science fiction became a way to get rich. Most of us didn't. But I never expected that, or even to make a living at it. When I started, there were only half a dozen authors who were writing science fiction as a full-time occupation, and some of them, like Heinlein, had other sources of income. And then the tie-in novels came along and the mainstream publishers lost economic interest in mid-list books (somewhat made up by the rise of small publishers), and the bean counters took over, shifting decisions about publication from editors to salespeople and accountants. But I always wrote what I wanted to write rather what someone wanted me to write or what I thought the market wanted, so I was neither disappointed nor disillusioned. I've spent a great deal of time on works that didn't accomplish what I hoped. But I've done what I wanted, lived the life I chose, and had some unexpected rewards. Recognition, and appreciation—I'm not sure having a bestseller would have changed that for the better.

Zebrowski: When H. G. Wells published his *The Discovery of the Future* in 1902, comparing the forward and backward looking attitude of mind, it seemed a novelty. The future, much less alternative futures, as we think of them today, did not exist. Wells argued for the cultivation of foresight as much as we lament the perfection of hindsight, and turn away from the responsibility that we make futures in which we arrive at every present.

Your motto of "Saving the world through science fiction" recognizes that science fiction encourages the forward looking attitude, and today envisions the idea of alternative futures through which to rehearse what we may make of ourselves.

Foresight seems a good cry, but some have objected to chaining the future to the mistakes of the past. Futures should not happen like a runaway train. Rehearse it, imagine it when it is still safe to do so, so that, as Ray Bradbury has suggested, we may prevent it.

Why should we think that we can do better at futures, when we clearly see so much wasted past?

Gunn: Much of that wasted past can be attributed to a dependence upon tradition rather than mistakes in imagining the future. For most of its history, humanity has looked to the past for answers about how to do things rather than to its likely outcome. This kind of resistance to change brings about contemporary problems, when traditional answers to earlier questions such as what should we do with our wastes, how can we harvest more animals, how can we get more arable land out of the forest, how many children must we have to see enough of them to survive to maturity, have unforeweek consequences. When conditions change attitudes survive and we are faced with pollution, over harvesting, over-cultivation, over-population, and now over-warming. Wells wrote about this, perhaps in the piece you mention, comparing the historical mind to the future-looking mind and ending with—I quote from memory: "One day in the long future of days Man will stand upon this Earth as one stands upon a footstool and reach out his hand among the stars."

My motto, let's save the world through science fiction, is a restatement of Wells's call for an "Open Conspiracy" of educated people of good will to create a better world. But it also implies that science fiction has a unique ability to shape people's minds and attitudes, as well as to lead to future thinking. I have proposed an experiment in neuroscience to explore the ways in which the brain responds to science fiction as compared with its response to other forms of fiction, because I believe that science fiction calls upon the rational forebrain rather than the emotional centers, and we ought to encourage the reading, writing, teaching, and discussion of science fiction as a way to a better world. As I suggested in my Transcendental trilogy, we need to fulfill our potential as humans if we are going to not only survive, as Faulkner said in his Nobel Prize acceptance remarks, but prevail. Science fiction may be our Transcendental Machine.

That may be naïve, but science fiction changed my life—as I document in my memoir *Star-Begotten* (another tribute to Wells)—and maybe, just maybe, it can change other people's lives and maybe even the world.

ABOUT GEORGE ZEBROWSKI

Science fiction writer Greg Bear calls George Zebrowski "one of those rare speculators who bases his dreams on science as well as inspiration." Zebrowski has published about a hundred works of short fiction, more than a hundred and forty articles and essays, and has written about science for *Omni Magazine*. His short fiction and essays have appeared in *Analog, Asimov's Science Fiction, Amazing Stories, The Magazine of Fantasy & Science Fiction, Science Fiction Age, Nature*, the *Bertrand Russell Society News, World Literature Today, Free Inquiry*, and other publications.

His best known novel is *Macrolife*, which Arthur C. Clarke described as "a worthy successor to Olaf Stapledon's *Star Maker.* It's been years since I was so impressed. One of the few books I intend to read again." *Library Journal* chose *Macrolife* as one of the one hundred best science fiction novels. His short fiction has been nominated for the Nebula Award and the Theodore Sturgeon Memorial Award. His novel *Stranger Suns* (1991) was a *New York Times* Notable Book of the Year.

The Killing Star (1995), written with scientist/author Charles Pellegrino, was described by *The New York Times Book Review* as "a novel of such conceptual ferocity and scientific plausibility that it amounts to a reinvention of that old Wellsian staple, [alien invasion]..." *Brute Orbits* (1998) was praised by Paul Di Filippo in *Asimov's Science Fiction*, who wrote that "Zebrowski never ceases to invest his individual characters with three-dimensional round-ness...Startling, sobering, provocative," while *Publishers Weekly* called this novel "boldly speculative." The book won the John W. Campbell Memorial Award for Best Novel of the Year. *Cave of Stars*, a novel that is part of his Macrolife mosaic, was published in 1999.

Other books include *Skylife*, an anthology edited by Zebrowski with Gregory Benford (2000), and the collection *Swift Thoughts* (2002). *Synergy SF: New Science Fiction*, the fifth volume of his Synergy series of original anthologies, was published in 2004. *Black Pockets and Other Dark Thoughts*, with an introduction by Howard Waldrop, came out in 2006, and a new edition of *Macrolife* was published in that year by Pyr Books, with an introduction by Ian Watson. Golden Gryphon published his horror novel *Empties* in 2009. *Sentinels In Honor of Arthur C. Clarke*, an anthology of fiction and nonfiction edited with Gregory Benford, was published in 2010 by Hadley Rille Books. His collection, *Decimated: Ten Science Fiction Stories*, with Jack Dann, was published in 2012 by Wildside Press.

ABOUT PAMELA SARGENT

Pamela Sargent has won the Nebula and Locus Awards and was honored in 2012 with the Pilgrim Award, given for lifetime achievement in science fiction and fantasy scholarship by the Science Fiction Research Association. Among her novels are *Cloned Lives, The Sudden Star, Watchstar, The Golden Space, The Alien Upstairs, Eye of the Comet, Homesmind, Alien Child, The Shore of Women, Venus of Dreams, Venus of Shadows*, and *Child of Venus*, as well as the alternative history *Climb the Wind* and the historical novel *Ruler of the Sky*. Her novel *Earthseed*, part of a trilogy that includes *Farseed* and *Seed Seeker*, is in development at Paramount Pictures. She also edited the *Women of Wonder* anthologies, the first collections of science fiction by women about women. Her short fiction has appeared in magazines, anthologies, and in her collections *Starshadows, The Best of Pamela Sargent, The Mountain Cage and Other Stories, Behind the Eyes of Dreamers and Other Short Novels, Eye of Flame, Thumbprints, Dream of Venus and Other Science Fiction Stories*, and *Puss in D.C. and Other Stories*. Her latest novel is *Season of the Cats*, out in hardcover in 2015 from Wildside Press with a trade paperback forthcoming in 2018. Her site is at www.pamelasargent.com.

www.ingramcontent.com/pod-product-compliance
Lightning Source LLC
Chambersburg PA
CBHW022051170626
46808CB00003B/1442